It's Still Complicated

...because I am still waiting

notionpress
.com

It's Still Complicated

...because I am still waiting

Chandra Kant Jaisansaria

notionpress.com

Notion Press

Old No. 38, New No. 6

McNichols Road, Chetpet

Chennai - 600 031

First Published by Notion Press 2015

ISBN: 978-93-5206-281-2

For the girl whom I loved, and who, for a brief but glorious time, loved me back.

Tujhe bhul jana hamare bas me nahin, kash hum tumhe wapis hamari zindagi me la pate.

Ek mauka hume aur diya hota tumne to shayad, tumhe apni zindagi bana paate…

Contents

ACKNOWLEDGEMENTS

My sincere thanks to the following people who have played an important role in the journey of writing and publishing this book.

My Mom who has always been there for me. You have always encouraged me to realize and see that I fulfill my dreams.

Gita Negi who has always been there as my mentor and showed me the path to fulfilling my dream of getting this novel published.

Vatsala Shrivastava you are my best friend, thank you for always being there to help me to complete this book. You were always concerned about this book and asking me to complete it and supported me when I lost interest in it many times in between. Thank you for cheering me up and being ready to discuss the ideas of getting it published and marketing it online. You have been my best buddy and a big support in completing this story. You have always been there for me whenever I needed you.

Saurabh Sarawagi my cousin, who read each and every part of the story and gave me continuous advice for the changes required in each part and feedback on all the chapters.

My relatives who always supported my idea of writing this book and realized my dream of becoming an author.

My friends who always cared for me when I was all alone with myself and keeping me alert on completing this book in time.

My Teachers and Professors because of whom I am what I am today; they are God for me and I will always love all of them and be thankful that they have helped shape me throughout this journey called life.

And finally, those who started this journey with me and left me in between and those who joined me in between and are still there for me.

I still remember your eyes
Beautiful like butterflies…
So silent so deep
Like an ocean which never cries…
You have a fabulous smile
Which has no price…
Your face, your style
Everything so nice…
Your heart is so pure
Like oceanic ice…
But without you,
My life is like a loser's dice…
When you are away
My heart dies…
My mind stops working
And my eyes, cry…
I hear your voice
Someday, sometimes…
But soon I realize
It's only a dream with open eyes…

06th January, 2014

It was a rainy day with so much fog that if one stepped outside, one's right hand could not see the other hand! At 2 pm in the afternoon, my phone rang and I kept my laptop aside, removed my quilt and left my warm and cozy bed even though I was feeling cold. I was quite worried and wondered to check if it was she who was calling. But no, it was some writer on the other side seeking time from me to meet me to get my story, a true love story which I always wanted to write on my own. "Sir, are you listening to me?? I am Kanika... I am a writer by profession and I could help you out if you agree... Sir..."

I disconnected the call and tears came rolling down from my eyes...

Kya khata thi hamari jo hum akele reh gae
Tere diye hue har gum, hum haske seh gae
Socha nahi tha kabhi ki tujhe chahenge is kadar
Tu aage nikal gai aur hum wahi reh gae...

In Search of Someone

After not getting admission in any of the colleges in Jaipur due to the limited number of seats and because of the rampant virus of our country called 'Corruption'; I was very dejected. Corruption, because people usually give a donation to the college and only then get admission for their children. But my Grandfather was an ethical and principled man; he refused to give a donation. He said to me, "Be someone who gets chosen by his talent, not money, every father may not have enough money to bribe." I got very discouraged with the 72% score in my mark sheet and felt like I was good for nothing.

It was sometime in August 2008 when I had come to Delhi for my college admission, I am bad at remembering the dates. I used to stay at my 'Mamaji's house in Rohini with my cousin Ravi. Ravi and I were best of cousins and he has a very calm and humorous nature; he never gets angry with me and I used to share a lot of things about my life with him. We both shared a single room and a single set of earphones while listening to the FM on my cell phone. We used to switch the channels the whole night till one of us fell asleep and if we were hungry late at night we were fond of eating Namkeens "*bhujia*'s". Of course in the morning Mami would know about it and shout at us. She would say you boys don't eat your dinner properly that's why you feel hungry at night. We used to laugh at people noticing their expression and we both are very good at mimicry. Does Ravi have a GF, no he dint! But he used to talk to one of his friend's Pooza, a lot, and of course I was jealous that I didn't have even a girl as a friend in Delhi.

Alas, it was the time when admissions were closed in every college except in the School Of Open Learning (Delhi University) and a few private colleges. Mamaji tried to somehow convince me to get admission in some private college and do my BBA from there. But I thought that I should get a degree from Delhi University instead of some random private college which would give me a degree of some other state university board. I knew I would not be able to enjoy my college life like all other regular college students, because SOL is not a regular college, but somehow I convinced myself to get admission in SOL. SOL also arranges some classes on Saturdays and Sundays for the students and I thought the attendance of SOL is important, so I started taking classes there too. There I made a friend... Amit Thakur, he was from somewhere in Himachal.

We became good friends; we used to hang out in college when the teacher was not there in the class, we used to bunk classes, sit outside Vishwa vidhyalaya Metro station and talk to each other about the girls coming out and going inside the metro station. Amit and I decided that whoever found a girlfriend first would take his girlfriend to the place where we used to sit during our class bunks, and would not leave his friend just because he got himself a GF.

We noticed something during one of our sessions. We saw a girl every Saturday; she used to come and sit in the park outside the metro station and help poor children by giving them eatables and to the pigeons as well. Amit and I were super excited to see her every Saturday. One day we both took a chance to talk to her and we started helping those poor children and the other beggars, just to show off to her how generous we were. She gave both of us such a lovely smile and it made our day. We repeated the same thing next Saturday, and again won a smile from her. This time we planned that next time one of us will take her cell number. But then we couldn't see her anymore, "*Kismet hi kharab hai yaar, chal ghar chal*," a frustrated Amit said. We lost interest in the SOL classes and as time passed by we stopped going to SOL and meeting each other. This is the time when he stopped being in my life. I don't even remember the first digit of his phone number. After all we have a tendency to forget old memories, which are not so important for us.

Then I started taking classes in NGPA, a private institute in Rohini, which was providing coaching to the undergraduate students for almost all the streams of subjects. A lot of students came on the first day of the institute's first session and a lot of beautiful girls too. There was a girl named Simran Kaur who was sitting on the last bench. She used to talk to every smart guy in my class. You know the type - those who had a nice physique, good looks, a bike and a good looking phone. Delhi is a place of show off. The better you represent yourself, the better your friend circle is. Maybe it was my thinking but somehow they were better than me and I had to convince myself that I was not capable enough to talk to her. But at the same time I knew that she was noticing me.

As the time passed, three months after the course started, in November, we finally got a PC at Mamaji's house and with an internet connection. I had my id on Orkut as 'Chandra Kant Jaisansaria', yes it was my original social networking id among the multiple id's which I made when I was in hostel.

In 2–3 days of making the Orkut id I started a search; searching for the first crush of my life - Priya. I found her profile, sent a friend request, and she accepted the friend request.

"Hi! How are you?" I said.

"Hi! I am fine what about you?" she replied.

"I am good. Where are you now days? After you left the school in class 7th, I couldn't see you even I went outside your house many times but..."

"I shifted to Calcutta with my family and I am doing my studies here," she replied.

I got her cell number and called her. We soon became the best of friends. We used to talk for hours and I told her that she was the first romantic 'Crush' of my life. She laughed!

"Oh really?" she replied.

"Yes! I always followed you after the school till you reach home. Sometimes I purposefully came outside your house in the evenings just to see you and I was a big, like a diehard fan of your smile. I even used to come to school on rainy days because I knew that you would come and I would be able to see you smile," I said.

Oh! My god, you are such a...: she replied.

"Such a what?" I said.

"Nothing, we are good friends now and we were destined to meet again," she said.

I was very happy to get her back in my life, I thought she might be the one who was meant for me and I promised her that I would always be her good friend and that I would always be there for her.

Then enters the so-called villains, a few of my former class mates from my hometown started sending her friend requests and messages and they even started teasing her about me. They somehow came to know that I was talking to her. I know why they did this, they did this just to separate us as she was the most beautiful girl from our school and everybody had once had a crush on her and they were jealous that she is talking to me! Priya got angry with me thinking that I had told them everything about us and she became very upset. That night I couldn't sleep a wink the entire night thinking that I had lost her again. But I couldn't let her go like this; after all, she was the one whom I liked the most. I still remember the day when I asked my mom "Mom can I marry a girl of some other caste?" and my mom replied "Inter-caste marriages are not allowed in our family, why do you like someone?" and I smiled.

The next day I called Priya and somehow convinced her that I didn't say anything to anyone and that I don't have any contact with anyone of them. "Why would I do so", I asked her, "I never want to lose you…" I took cell numbers of those idiots from her and called them up. I told them to stop disturbing Priya. They all came on a conference call together and told me that, it was because of me that Priya was not replying to any of them. They threatened me and told me that if she did not talk to them, they would beat me whenever I was back in town. I was afraid of them because there were many and I was alone, but somehow I was happy that after all I was clear of my charges and if Priya was with me then I could handle them. I was ready to get a beating from all of them but I vowed that I would not let them disturb her again. Both of us blocked all of them on our phones and Orkut and soon they were not able to disturb us.

23rd January, 2009

It was my birthday and I was damn excited to celebrate it in Delhi. After Priya wished me 'Happy Birthday' at 12 o'clock sharp at midnight, everyone else at my home did the same. I was happy to get a call from Priya, It made my day thinking that I was so important for her that she was awake till 12, just to wish me. As soon as the phone stopped ringing and everyone had slept I sat up on my bed quietly. I was unable to sleep in the complete silence; suddenly, my mind had no thoughts running through it but a tear came rolling down my cheeks. I was crying because somewhere deep down I was hurt, it was a feeling of being alone in the presence of many.

Shayad hum kisi se keh na sake
Par koi to hogi aisi jiske bina hum reh na sake
Wo aae humse milne kabhi kabhi
Aur hum har pal uskii raahen taken...

Megha

As I have said before, I am bad at remembering dates One day while going through the friend suggestions on my Orkut page I wondered if I could search for Megha, who had become my friend during my time in class 8th. I clicked on the search tab and wrote 'Megha Jain' their but I couldn't find her. I don't know why, maybe it was my destiny which made me do so, I wrote Megha Agarwal on the search tab and my eyeballs were stuck on an incomplete profile, among all those results. Her profile did not have any DP, it said she was from Pitampura and was a student of DAV school. She was just 3 kms away from me, and I couldn't stop myself from sending her a friend request but instead of sending a friend request I left her a message "Hey! I am new in Delhi and I don't have many friends here, unlike other guys of Delhi, I would not disturb you ever if you are not interested but I promise that I will never hurt you. I just want a simple friendship with you, if you don't mind".

Late that night I went on my bed and kept asking myself 'Why'? Why would I send a friend request to someone who doesn't even know me and that too to a girl having no DP on her profile? I called up Priya and told her about all those things and she dint react to this. Maybe because she was not my girlfriend. The next day when I came back home after my classes, I was in a hurry to check whether she had replied to my message or not.

Yes! There was a reply, she said "Hi! I haven't got any friend request from you yet." "Oh I tried it; but I am not able to send it because of some problem in my PC. Would you please send me a friend request"?

I got a friend request and added her.

"Hi! How are you?" I said.

"Hello! I am fine and you?" she replied

"So, you don't have a DP on your profile," I said.

"You too! Don't have a DP on your profile!" she replied.

"Umm, I don't look smart enough and I never get photos clicked unless it is required for some paper work," I replied.

"Never mind, friends should have a beautiful heart, the face really doesn't matter," she said.

"Yes! You are right, and I hope we carry on our friendship for a very long time," I said.

She was suddenly offline now, and I got a bit worried about what would have happened to her that she had gone without saying a good bye. I kept thinking about the conversation between us the next day, I was worried. I kept thinking if our conversation had gone ok? Did I say something which she may have not liked and went offline? The questions were hitting my head hard from inside. I became restless, and I was going online again and again to check whether she is there. I was trying to figure out the other possibilities because of which she must have gone offline.

Suddenly a light flashed on my screen indicating that I had received a new message. "Hi! Sorry I went offline without a Bye, my mom called me up to help her in the kitchen," my new friend Megha had messaged me. There she was… my heartbeat slowed down and I relaxed.

"It's okay, there is no sorry and no thank you in friendship… and by the way in which class do you study?" I asked her to continue the conversation.

I am in class 11 and I have my exams next month and I will not be able to come online so frequently, if you don't mind can I have your cell number…" she said to me.

Its 9…, when can I expect to get a call from you?" I asked.

Very soon! Right now I have to go, bye, take care…"

She went offline and I was very happy, I called up Priya and shared the conversation with her and she dint react, as I was expecting her to react. I thought she might be in love with me and would get angry with me. But she did not, as she considered me just a friend. Even I did not bother about her now as I was happy that for the first time in my life a girl had asked for my cell number.

Three days had passed since Megha took my cell number and there was no call, no text, and no message on Orkut. I was worried but I knew the reason behind it, I was just waiting for her call so intensely that I couldn't keep my eyes off of my cell phone. The third day my phone rang in the evening, it was an unknown number and it looked like a VIP number. I felt that it must be her.

"Hello!" I received the call.

"Hi! It's Megha,"

This was her voice; it was damn cute like the voice of a child, and my ear drums could not believe that they had heard something which would immediately give someone a feeling of relaxation. I felt like my heart had slowed down, the time had stopped and I could feel like a new blood was circulating through my veins; it was as if I could only hear her voice. Her melodious voice could have made me do anything for her. I felt like I was hypnotized by her voice.

"Are you there! Are you listening! Hello..."

"Yes, I am listening; after all I was waiting for your call for the last 3 days..." I said in a slow tone.

"Oh! So sorry, I was busy studying and right now I have got time to talk to you because I am on the way to my institute for my accounts class," she replied hurriedly, walking towards the institute.

"Ok. So you take tuitions to study accounts; I was very good in accounts in school and scored 72% in the subject," I replied getting confused about what to talk to her.

"That's nice, what was your average score in 10th& 12th?" she asked.

My mouth suddenly felt dry and I choked, I couldn't utter a word thinking, "*Beta ab tu gaya, ise sach pata chala to ye kya sochegi*?" But somehow I forced myself to speak the truth because it was a new friendship which I couldn't start from a lie.

"I scored 55% in my 10th and 72% in the 12^{th,}" I said in a sad tone, "I hope that you don't mind making me your friend, even if I am not good in my studies,"

"No ways yaar, marks doesn't matter, even I got 47% in the 10th and what matters is your behavior with me; after all everyone is not born with intelligence," she sweetly accepted me for what I was and she hung up the phone saying that she had reached. But she did promise to call me later.

I was expecting a call from her while she would go back home from the tuitions, but she did not call me up, and instead messaged me and said, "Hi! I am going back home but won't be able to call you, but we can chat through sms..."

"Hi! No problem, by the way, if you don't mind me asking. Do you have a boyfriend?" I know I jumped very soon on this topic but I could not stop myself from asking her.

"No, I don't believe in all this, do you have a girl friend?" she asked.

"No, as of now I don't have any. But I have a best friend Priya with whom I share almost everything," I said.

"Where do you stay in Delhi?" she asked me.

"I stay in Rohini, and basically I am from Rajasthan and my family lives in Rajasthan only," I added to keep the conversation going.

"So you stay in a PG?" she asked.

"No, I stay at my Mamaji's house," I said.

"What do you do?" she asked.

"I am currently doing my B.Com from SOL and go for tuitions of some subjects in NGPA," I replied.

"Ok. Will talk to you tomorrow as I am tired and have to help mom with her kitchen work. Catch you later. Good Night!" she said.

"Good Night? I mean come on... the conversation just started and..." but I had to reply to her Good night and wait for the next day to talk to her.

Now I know you might be thinking what the hell has happened to Priya? Where is she? Did I talk to her also?

Yes. I talked to her but the conversation between us became less and less, day by day and soon it was an old story for me.

The Night was very long; time was so slow that if I could have thrown a needle in the night it would have dropped on the land in the morning. But luckily I had Ravi with me, with whom I shared everything. He was very surprised to see that I that I had made a friend through Orkut. According to him, this was only possible in the movies.

Unhone hath bhi nahi badhaya tha
Hum unki taraf badhte chale gae
Raaten hui lambi
Din ghat te chale gae
Aakhir hua wahi
Jin galiyo me hum jana chahte the ek arse se
Un galiyo ki taraf hum badhte chale gae…

"Bus Train *aur Ladki, in teen ke pichhe kabhi mat bhagna.*" I have heard this many times and somehow I stopped myself from sending her a text the next day. Maybe because I knew she was in school and that she would call me in the evening while going for her tuition.

And as expected the call came in the evening. This time she told me that she had a cousin named Sakshi. Sakshi seemed very beautiful the way she described her and as I was single and maybe looking for a girlfriend, she told me that Sakshi would be perfect for me to get into a relationship with. I was not at all interested in Sakshi as I had started liking Megha, so I told her that I was not looking for a girlfriend as I had already started liking someone. When she asked me "Who is she?" I somehow changed the topic and I asked her to meet me, so that we could get to know each other better. She agreed to meet me and she said that she would also bring Sakshi with her, as she was not comfortable in meeting me alone. We decided to meet at Pitampura Metro station the next day.

I was very happy and damn excited to meet her; I ate my dinner hurriedly and went to the bed early that day, because I somehow wanted, time to run fast and waited for the day to come. But I couldn't sleep the whole night as I spent all the time thinking of her. I don't know when I fell asleep... but I knew that I was still thinking of her.

09th February, 2009 (The First Meeting)

My phone rang, and as expected it was her.

"Good Morning! Are you still sleeping?" she asked me.

"Good Morning. I don't know when I fell asleep, but I am happy that it's you who woke me up,"

"Really! Just woke up and I called you to confirm that we are going to meet today,"

"Yes, I remember. I am just getting ready, by what time you will be at Pitampura Metro station?"

"I'll be there at 11 am,"

I got up, and got ready before everybody else at home woke up. Mami was surprised to see me ready and asked me whether I had any tuition that day. I told her that I had a very important class and had to leave without taking my breakfast and I left home quickly. While travelling to Pitampura on the Metro, my mind had several questions, like:

What if she is a fat looking girl?

What if she blinks repeatedly? Or...

Stop! I said to my mind, she is my friend, I like her, and I would accept her for whatever she is.

I reached Pitampura Metro station and waited for her, it was just 10:30 am, and I called her and asked where she was?

She said she was at Kohat Enclave Metro station, and by mistake she told me to come to Pitampura Metro station. I had to take a token again to reach Kohat and wait for some more time to meet her. I got very much excited; I ran towards the counter and took the token for Kohat. I don't know what happened to me that I was running like someone has left his dog behind me. I was running toward the first coach of the metro because this coach will first enter the Kohat Metro Station. I boarded the metro and as soon as I reached Kohat I called her to ask where she was. She said she was at Gate no.3 waiting for me and I went running towards gate no. 3. But as soon as I reached to the stairs I was very nervous. Time had stopped by now, everything has slowed down, sunrays were directly falling on my face like a spotlight falls on a performer during his performance, disallowing me to see her from upstairs. I saw two girls standing downstairs and looking at me. I went downstairs slowly wondering - is this Megha and is that Sakshi? If yes, what's going on in their heads, looking at me? I got more conscious at every step going towards them. I took my cell phone out to confirm that this is Megha and she waved her hand to tell me that there is no need to call, it was her.

I was now standing right in front of her, she was looking dazzling in her black top and blue slim fit jeans, and she has untied long black and silky hair which I dreamt about. She had a beautiful smile which could win thousands of hearts in a second and no one could ever get tired looking at her. Her figure could give competition to any of the actresses in Bollywood. She was a perfect match for any of the guys looking out for a decent, simple and innocent looking girl. Her face reflected her cuteness and simplicity of nature. I was lost looking into her eyes that I couldn't even give a look towards Sakshi.

Before I could gather some confidence and utter a word she said "Hi! I am Megha and this is Sakshi!"

"Hi!"

"Sorry! I thought this is Pitampura Metro Station... sorry to keep you waiting there at Pitampura,"

"No worries, after all I have reached and we are here. By the way you have reached before time and I thought I would have to wait for you people to come,"

"Umm, this is the first time where I have reached before time otherwise I am always late," She said laughing.

"Ohk! So, I will have to wait if I had to meet you again in future," I smiled.

"Maybe", she said; "Anyways we have to leave now as we have to go to the market and buy some stuff for us; will see you some other day,"

"Bye," I said.

"Don't say bye, say see ya. I don't like the word 'Bye'. When we say bye, we don't know when we will meet next, but if we say see you, it means we are meeting very soon!"

"See ya! I said.

She went off, even as my eyes followed her.

I didn't want her to go, even though I had just met her. I felt like I should take her home and keep looking at her till the end of this world, I felt like she was the only one for me; the one I had dreamt about, my dream girl. I had heard someone say "When you are with your loved one, time runs so fast that you don't even recognize it, but when she is away from you the time goes so slowly that every minute is like an hour..." This was the time when I fell in love with her deeply.

I went to the institute to attend the classes, but I don't remember if I studied anything that day. Everyone was busy looking at me doing awkward things, like smiling again and again, putting the pen on the desk and suddenly start writing something, looking at phone and reading her messages over and again, the teacher did not bother looking at me as she dint wanted the class to get disturbed. I went home and I was a completely different CK by now. I was going to the PC switching it on, then off, then walking in hall, again going to the PC and again switching it on and off. I became restless, I dint even remember that I haven't had food since the morning and it was 9 pm in the night. I waited eagerly for Ravi to come. He came and I explained everything to him. He made me realize that I was in love and he was damn surprised to see me like this.

I went to bed and I messaged her that I wanted to meet her again, I don't know what was going on in her mind, but she said ok, and that she would plan to meet me very soon. She explained that she was a bit tired today because of the shopping and would talk to me tomorrow.

"See you," she said.

"See you!" I replied.

The next day we dint talk as we both were busy with our classes, but I called her in the evening.

"Hey! I wanted to ask you a question since we met, how do I look to you?" I asked her.

"Hi! You look okay! No so smart but better than any average guy, and blow what I expected you to look like,"

I had mixed emotions hearing this but still said to her "Okay.".

She asked me the same question and also asked me "How was Sakshi?"

"You looked damn impressive" I told her, "you were above expectations, if I had to tell you what you look like, I would write a poem."

"Seriously?" she asked, "Do you write poems?"

"Yes, I do sometimes when I am in a very good or very bad mood, it depends,"

"Okay! Nice, by the way what about Sakshi?"

"I dint pay much attention to her, she looked pretty but I was lost in your eyes…," I smiled.

"She looks better than me, she is…"

"Umm… you look better than her if you ask me and I am happy to have you as a friend," I said to her.

I could feel the smile on her face.

"Listen!", she interrupted our conversation suddenly.

"I have to go to school tomorrow, so see you. Good Night,"

"Good Night."

12th February, 2009 (The Proposal)

It was a regular day, we both had our classes and were busy with our respective schedules, so I waited till the evening to call her. I called, but she dint picked up the phone. I was wondering why she dint pick up the call. Luckily, I got a call from her very soon.

"Hey! Sorry I was busy with some household stuff with my mom; I saw your call when I got free so we can talk now,"

"Hi! If you don't mind I want you to just listen to me for a while and leave everything you are doing right now…"

"Why? Is everything okay?" she asked me in a surprised tone.

"Yes it is, but I never knew I was going to feel this way. I'm not sure how to do it, but I have to tell you what's on my mind so here goes…"

"What happened? What do you want to say?"

"Megha – Since we met I am not able to walk straight on the road, my eyes keep searching you everywhere. My dreams have nothing in them except your smiling face; in every text book it's you, I go blank while studying in class, everyone says I am lost, but I think I have found myself in you. I am lost in your eyes as if they have hypnotized me, I don't even bother about what everyone thinks of me, I'll sleep without having food but will not be able to sleep without talking to you. Every second without you is like an hour for me, if god would have given me a chance to redeem my million good works against the one thing which I want in my life, I would only ask for you. What I am trying to say is **I Love You** and I live for you sweetheart, will you be my Life forever?"

There was a complete silence from both sides… I was afraid of losing her, thousands of questions started running in my mind… I guess it was too early to propose to her, but I didn't know what was happening on the other side… After a long pause she said…

"Look, you are such a true and decent guy, every other girl on this planet would never say no, as you are worth loving. But my family has different thoughts; they are orthodox and they would never allow me to have a love marriage. I don't have enough courage to tell them about you, believe me they would not like it even if they saw me talking to you. You don't know them they are very strict and will never let it happen. I am sorry, I can't say yes…"

Suddenly it seemed like everything in my life had fallen apart. I felt like the blood had stopped running in my vessels, that the heart was not pumping and had stopped beating, the silence was killing me. It was a feeling which broke me from inside. I felt so weak that I was not able to hold my phone. Somehow I gathered the courage to speak and could utter the next few words…

"**I Love You** and will always do, I'll become everything which your father wants me to. I'll try everything to convince your family, if you are not able to tell them I'll tell them that we love each other and will find out a better way to make it an arranged marriage somehow. Please say yes… please…

"Sorry I can't," and she hung up the phone.

I was sad, I told Ravi about it, he somehow tried to make me smile but I couldn't smile. He knew where I was and what I was feeling but he didn't have any choice, and neither did I. I spent the whole night crying and thinking about her. I felt like maybe she would never talk to me after this. It was as if I had lost my control of all the senses, I felt like I was sleeping on a death bed having a lot to say but I dint have anyone to hear it. I was feeling like I am lost in a cage having mirrors everywhere and don't have any escape from it. I couldn't hold my tears but after a while my eyes got tired of taking out the water from them.

13th February, 2009

Ravi woke me up; he was very worried and asked me to repeat the whole conversation which I had with Megha last night. I repeated every word as it is, like a tape recorder. He came to a conclusion after listening to the conversation, he said to me – "Look bro, she loves you. All you need to do is make her emotional and fall for you and that job is mine now..."

He took my phone and sent a message to Megha.

"Hi! This is Ravi, his cousin. He couldn't sleep the whole night, he cried a lot He loves you so much that while thinking about you he burnt one of his fingers while boiling the milk in kitchen. He seriously loves you and I don't know why, but he is mad on you..."

14th February, 2009 (The Valentine's Day)

She called me up in the evening,

"Hey!"

"Hi!"

"I am sorry to hurt you, I just called you to say, that... that... **I Love You,"**

"I was just worried that I would lose you, but sorry I don't love you..." I said rudely and I disconnected the call.

Surprised?? Why did I do this?? and that too on Valentine's Day.

There were two reasons behind it.

One, I wanted to see that if she was also dying for me.

Second, I wanted to propose to her and to hear a 'Yes' from her side. I mean a guy always like to propose and a girl accepts it, right...

I know it sounds silly but above all I wanted her to wait for me, after all **Love** gets intensified in the absence or wait of someone.

16th February, 2009 (The Final Proposal)

It's been 2 days since we talked to each other, I was wondering why there was no call from her side for the last 2 days. I had few questions in my mind...

Was she angry with me?

Maybe she didn't want to talk to me because she thinks I have broken her heart by refusing her proposal?

She might be sad and crying because I hurt her. This was also possible, right?

Maybe she was dying to talk to me, but she wants me to call her first?

I couldn't resist myself from calling her; I was dying to listen to her voice and after all so I gave up and I called her

"Hey!"

"Hi!"

"I am Sorry."

"It's ok..."

"Look, I dint say Yes because I wanted you to feel how much you love me and I wanted you to know how much you can get hurt when you hear a 'No'... I tried to be funny at the wrong time... But like I said **I Love You**!"

She said "I Love You too!"

I felt like I was bent on my knees in front of her and giving her a red rose; I imagined that she was smiling and accepted my rose speaking those 3 magical words which I was dying to hear. I was lost somewhere and a tear of happiness touched my cheeks. I then requested her to meet me as I was dying to see her again and wanted to get lost in her deep, innocent eyes.

She promised me that she would soon make a plan to meet but suddenly she was silent now.

I couldn't understand her silence and I asked, "What happened?"

"Nothing," she said.

"Are you not happy with this?"

"Yes I am, it's just..."

"It's just??"

"I burnt my hand the other day because you were hurt, and it's paining..."

"Did you apply medicine on it?"

"Yes, I did."

Okay! I want you to promise me one thing today..."

"What?"

"You will never hurt yourself hereafter, and you will always take care of yourself. Promise???"

"Promise,"

Okay, now go and take some rest, we will talk tomorrow, Good Night. I Love you..."

"Love you too."

I had mixed emotions this time; on the one hand I was happy that she had accepted the proposal and that she cares for me so much that she hurt herself when I was hurt, and on the other hand I was sad that because of me she hurt herself and I never wanted her to get hurt.

Finally, we both were a couple now and I know that we were going to be in a lifelong relationship together which I would never allow to end. My happiness had no end; I was feeling like I had just won the world cup. I was excited to tell Ravi about this, I shared this with him as soon as he reached home and he was very happy to see me smile. That night I was listening to the melodious songs of Aatif Aslam, my all time favorite on FM.

One to One

17th February, 2009

"Good morning! Sweetheart!" I started the day with a text message to her.

"Good morning,"

"I am very happy to have you in my life and I am very excited to meet you again,"

"We will meet very soon. I have to go to school, what's your plan for the day?"

"Well I have some classes, but no use; I know I'll be lost in you completely,"

Hehehe..." You are so cute to be in love with. I have to get ready will call you in the evening,"

"Okay! Love you!"

"Love you too,"

One thing I appreciate about her is that she is very much expert in hiding her feelings, she sometimes mischievously hides her feelings just to tease me, and sometimes to hear something which she wanted me to speak. But I somehow made her confess what she was hiding. She wanted to say **'I Love You'** but she couldn't express it and I had to make her speak those three magical words which I wanted to hear so badly.

In the evening she called me and gave me good news, she had made a plan to meet me; she told me that she has made up a plan for a movie with Sakshi, her friend Sagar and me for Friday. Though I wanted to meet her alone this time but I knew she might not be feeling comfortable enough to meet me alone or she might have not got any other excuse to go out of her home without a chaperone. So I had to say yes. My happiness seemed to multiply I was feeling like I was on cloud 9; for the heaven's sake release the movie tomorrow I can't wait till Friday, I said to god looking at the sky.

She then started asking me about my family, like who all are in my family and what do they do. I explained about my Grand Father as the head of the family whose every word is a "*Patthar ki Lakeer*", he is the man of principles and our family is a joint family. My father and Uncle are the only two brothers and they followed every instruction of their mom (my grandmother) and then I have one brother Dinesh, who studies in school and then my uncle has three children, Divya, Manish and Happy. Happy is my darling, a little baby doll and I love her most in my family.

"Do you Love her more than me?" she asked innocently.

"Yes, but may be in future I'll love you both equally," I said.

She Laughed and said "I too Love Tani and Sana di more than you,"

I wondered who they were and I asked her about her family.

"I have my Ammaji (grandmother) as the head of the family and my Father and Tauji are the only two sons. I have one elder sister Kavya and a younger brother Ronit. Tauji has two children Aadi Bhaiya and Sana Di. Tani is Aadi Bhaiya's daughter."

"Okay!" I said thinking about the similarities in our families.

Soon I heard a voice; it was Mami, calling me for the dinner, oh shit! I had to go and I was not in any mood to disconnect the call but I had to.

"Bye, Love you will talk to you tomorrow. Mami is calling me,"

"Ok. Love you too. Take Care. See you."

20th February, 2009

Finally, it was the day of the 'Second Meeting' with her. I called up Dipesh to drop me to the movie hall as I did not have any vehicle of my own that time. He dropped me there and I introduced him to Megha. He then left me there and went home. Megha then introduced me to Sagar, Sakshi's friend, who was 5'6" with a good physique and he had a very nice sense of dressing. Delhi 6, It was my first movie with Megha. We went inside the hall and were sitting in the back row corner side; I sat in the corner and next to me were Megha, then Sakshi and then her friend. It was Abhishek Bachchan as the leading hero in the movie with Sonam Kapoor as the lead actress. Except for this I don't remember anything, as I was lost in her eyes again. She was watching the movie and I was watching her, I wanted to hold her hand, but my heart and mind started a battle between them…

Stop! Don't do it Sakshi is sitting next to her, my Mind said.

Shut up you idiot she is busy watching the movie I want to feel her.

You should not do it, what if Megha feels awkward about this??

No, she will not. She loves me and maybe she is waiting for me to hold her hand. Just shut up and let me hold her hand, and my heart won the battle.

I took my hand to the same arm rest where she had her hand and touched her palm with my fingers and then slowly holding her hand, I smiled. She was okay with it. We both were busy in looking at each other, ignoring everything around us, the song 'Masakali' was the icing on the cake. She smiled looking at me and I smiled too. We both were so lost in each other that we didn't knew when the movie got over.

Finally it was the time to go home, I said goodbye to Sagar who was always smiling, and then bye to Sakshi and a special 'See Ya' to Megha. Remembering her views about the difference between 'Bye' and 'See Ya'. She smiled and got inside the car, and I was waiting for her to turn back and give me a sweet innocent smile, and there she was… she turned her face and gave me a smile… all I could do was see her till the car was out of reach and wait for my next meeting with her.

I reached home and was waiting for her call; maybe because she was busy with her family, she called me only later on in the evening.

"Hey!"

"Hi!"

"How was the movie?" she asked.

"The Movie? I mean, I didn't pay any attention to the movie, for the whole three hours. I was just busy looking at you sweet heart..."

I know she was smiling, I could hear her silence.

"So..."

"So??"

"So... what's in your mind now?"

"I Love You. This was the best day of my life sweetheart, I wish I could spend my whole life watching at you and looking at your smiling face. I hope we marry each other very soon and live the rest of our lives in each other's arms."

"I Love You too... you are very sweet,"

"And?

"And... And... you have a very sweet voice, so much so that I want to hear it more and more..." she said praising my voice.

"Oh! Did you like my voice, thank you, but I never noticed that my voice was good,"

"*Achha Ji*..."

Hmm...

"When you smile, you look very cute..."

"Hahaha...I am not a kid sweetheart!" I was confused about what to say, I mean it was the first time she was expressing her views towards me...

"Ok, now we will talk later, I have to help mumma with her work. Good Night,"

Hearing this I was very angry with her elder sister Kavya, Can't she help her mom in the household work, why is it always Megha?? But I had to say 'Love you' and let her go.

"I Love You!"

"Love you too." and she disconnected the call running toward the kitchen...

10th April, 2009 (One-to-One)

After waiting the whole month of March because of her exams for the 11th Standard, this was the day when we met 'One-to-one' for the first time. The place was Japanese Park, which is also known as Lovers Point, because on weekdays, a lot of couples can be seen there, walking hand in hand or doing their love making scenes.

I was waiting for her outside the park, it was a sunny day and there was not much rush in the park. Finally she came in a rickshaw which she must have hired from the Rohini West Metro Station. She was looking stunning in her sky blue top and black jeans. We went inside the park and made ourselves comfortable near a beautiful pond. I was looking at her continuously, and could not take my eyes off her smiling face. I was captivated by those strands of her beautiful silky hair falling on her shoulders covering her ears and cheeks, and she was moving her hair behind her ear looking at me.

To break the silence and to distract me from looking at her constantly, she asked me, "Did I come late?"

"A couple of minutes, but it doesn't matter. I can wait for you for my whole life," I said, helping her hair behind her ear this time.

"What do you like the most in me?" she asked.

"I like your hair, and I feel like... I feel like putting my head on your lap and getting the shadow of your lovely hair on my face..."

There was complete silence once again, I was looking at her, and felt myself spellbound in her beauty and could not resist myself holding her hand and saying, "Will you be mine forever?"

She smiled and answered… "Yes I'll be…"

We both kept on looking at each other madly in love for a few more minutes and then I asked her about her school and her friends…

And we know when a girl starts speaking on something which she likes or dislikes the most; it's difficult for us to stop her. She kept on telling me about her school, her friends, her cousins and I don't remember a single word of what she had explained to me in the last one hour, as I was lost in her and at the end she suddenly asked me, 'Isn't it so?"

"What?" I asked showing her that I was paying attention to what she had, but I missed the last line…

"I am getting late and my mumma would shout if I don't reach home in time…"

"Oh! Then let me drop you at the metro station…"

I dropped her at the metro station and took the same rickshaw to my apartment. I called her after few hours and said… I have written something for you.

"Written something?? Oh the poem, which you promised to me that you would write for me…"

"Yes, just check your mail,"

"I am just checking it, hang on…" and she read it aloud on the phone…

The Girl I Love

I love a girl
For me she is precious than a pearl
I love her beauty
As she is my cutie
I love her charm
Feel lonely without her arms
I love her innocently
She believes it decently
I love her hair
So silky, so fair
I love her eyes
Beautiful like butterflies
I love her lips
Soft like roses leaves
She is just like a doll
Like a gold found in the mine of coal
She is my princess
Often like to wear new dresses
She is my life
And I pray to god that
She becomes my wife…

"Oh my god! Oh my god! Oh my god! You are so sweet and I love you for this, awesome... muaaahhh..." I could hear her kiss and she was very happy.

I felt very good that she liked the poem and moreover in her happiness lies, my happiness. I asked her, "Would you do me a favor in return?"

"Yes, tell me what could I do for you?"

"Send me your pic, wearing the same sky blue top which you were wearing today..."

She said okay! And sent the pic through MMS.

I was very happy to have her in my life and finally we could meet each other alone and spend quality time with each other. I saved that picture in my mobile and in my eyes too. I kept on watching the picture the whole night and wondered how beautiful a girl could be. Does god have a special machine which made her so beautiful that anyone could fall for her? I was rewinding the meeting and playing it again and again in my mind. I don't remember whether I could sleep that night or not, but I am damn sure that this time I had found the girl whom I would marry and spend my whole life with her.

We both were behaving like any other couple in this world. Wishing each other "Good Morning" chatting on messages all the time, calling each other when we had no one around us. Peeping in on each other's life, guiding and sometimes, ordering each other to do or not to do some things.

One day when I called Megha, her elder sister Kavya received the call; this was my first conversation with her. Thereafter we had many conversations between us and quite frequently; we both shared a lot of things with each other and then we became good friends. After few days we met each other and I was happy that I had someone who knew that both of us were going around and would help Megha and me when we need someone's support. Megha knew this and she was okay with it. Meanwhile Megha also told me that she has come to know about her cousin Sakshi having a boyfriend named Lalit, and we laughed a lot remembering the day, when Megha told me to go out with Sakshi as she would have been perfect for me. But we both were happy that we had another couple with us who would be hanging around with us and maybe accompany us to movies and other fun outings.

28th May, 2009 (Megha's Birthday)

We had already planned to go to the Cross River mall in Shahdara to celebrate Megha's birthday. Megha, Sakshi and I travelled by metro towards Shahdara, and Kavya, Lalit and his friends joined us there at the mall.

After cutting the birthday cake and celebrating Megha's birthday, we all went for the 'Scary House Ride'. I had never been on any such ride in my life, it was the first time. After buying the tickets, we went inside the so-called 'Scary House'; it was a dark room having a different kind of lighting and smoky atmosphere inside. There were a lot of stairs after every 10 meters or so and different kinds of artificial trees by the sides of the foot path on which we were walking. The best part was that every few seconds something happened which scared us. Sometimes it was a guy without a head, or sometimes it's was a witch coming out from a coffin and running behind us.

Suddenly it was an artificial snake which someone threw on both of us, me and Megha. She held my hand tightly, and that was the moment when we forgot everything and were just walking hand in hand towards the exit without being afraid of anything. It was just like a movie scene where a boy and girl confess their love for each other in front of their families and walk hand in hand and say 'We want to marry each other and we want to live and die in each other's arm no matter what happens!.

Soon the party was over and it was the time to go home. I, Megha and Sakshi travelled to Pitampura by metro and Kavya, Lalit and his friends left on their own conveyance. After seeing off Megha and Sakshi, I went home. This time I had two thoughts in my mind, on the one hand I was happy to see her smile and happy but on the other hand I was sad because I wanted to hug her, but I couldn't.

The Blackest Day of My Life

13th August, 2009

It was 8:30 in the morning when I was sleeping but I could hear voice of my Mamaji's friend, who had come to our home early that day. I tried to open my eyes to see him but I was feeling very sleepy and couldn't open my eyes and fell asleep again. Suddenly Mamaji's phone rang and the call was from my home at Rajasthan. I couldn't hear what they were talking on the phone but somehow I could grasp that there was some bad news. Mami woke me up and told me to get ready without taking a bath as I had to go to Rajasthan immediately. I asked my Mamaji about the reason behind it, he said that my Grandfather was not well and was hospitalized, so I had to go.

I was confused after hearing this because first of all, there was no good hospital in Sardar Shahar (my hometown). Secondly, my Grandfather was a well-built who was 6ft tall and I couldn't remember him being unwell. Though he used to take some medicines for asthma, but looking at him nobody could ever say he was unwell.

I got into the taxi with two of my Mamaji's, Shiv Mamaji and Surendra Mamaji. I sent a message to Megha that our date for that day was cancelled as I had to go Home. I had a plan to meet Megha as I came back to Delhi, just two days back, after a vacation of 15 days which I spent in Rajasthan itself. Megha did not reply, maybe she was sleeping by that time so I had to ask Ravi to call Megha after a few hours and explain her about the situation.

I was worried about my Grandfather; suddenly Shiv Mamaji asked Surendra Mamaji, when did he die? Hearing this I started crying my heart out. It was a journey of 5 hours from Delhi to my hometown. I was very sad, my Grandfather was everything for me and my family, whatever I am today was just because of him. He started his work life first earning to support his family as a truck driver and then became rich because of his hard work. I remember the days which I spent with him and how he completed each and every wish of mine.

I started recollecting my last meeting with my Dadaji, when he asked me two questions, "Are you going to Delhi tomorrow? Who will give me medicine from tomorrow?" Which I couldn't answer and while going to Delhi that day he said bye, which I have never heard from him earlier.

Now I realized why Megha always used to tell me never to say bye to anyone because we are not sure that whether we are going to meet that person again or not. That's why she used the words 'See Ya', instead of 'Bye'. If we say 'See Ya', there is a hope that we would meet again.

I reached home at 5pm that day, my eyes were filled with tears and I couldn't see anything except my home, I went inside and saw my Grandfather lying in middle of the courtyard. I never saw him so silent and his face was lifeless; my eyes searched for my father. I ran towards my father and hugged him and cried a lot. People who were gathered at my home took my Grandfather to the Mukti Dham and after the Kriya Karm they all went home, but me and my family were left alone, to cry and to feel sad about Dadaji.

I couldn't eat anything that day, whatever I was given to eat would come out of my throat and I felt like nothing was good to taste when you have just lost your loved one. Megha being an innocent and caring girl didn't call me that day, no doubt she was worried about me but she wanted me to call her when things would settle down. I called her the next day; she asked me the reason behind this miss-happening. I explained to her he died because of the heart attack in the morning and I started crying. This was the first time when she saw me crying and there was nothing which she could do about this. She innocently asked me to take care of everyone at home and myself too. She was worried about me and my family and she made me promise her that I would eat properly and take care of everyone at home. Those 12 days were the toughest days of my life and she was a great support for me. She used to call me once every few hours and ask me to take care of everyone at home. My love for her multiplied that time, because in this type of situation you understand who is your true friend and who is not.

I remember the day when I had a healthy argument with my Grandfather about my marriage. He had said that he would get me a girl who will have three qualities: one, she will be less educated than me. Two, she will be poorer than me. Three, she would be from a village, and laughed. Then I said, I would marry a girl who will be completely different from this. One, she would be equally educated. Two, she would be from a rich family. Three, she would be from a city. I remember that by the time when we had that conversation I was already in a relationship with Megha and she possesses all the qualities which I wanted in my dream girl. I could not tell my Grandfather about Megha as he was very strict in all these matters, but now I will never be able to tell him about her.

27th August, 2009 (Delhi)

I came back to Delhi to continue my studies, leaving my family behind. This is the phase of life where we don't feel good about anything. My Mamaji, Mami and Ravi gave me a lot of emotional support, they tried to keep me happy all the time and they never left me alone. They could very well understand the pain I was going through and I was glad to have them with me always.

Megha asked me to meet her at Kohat Enclave Metro station, the place where we met for the first time. She planned to meet me after her school and Kohat was on the way to her home. I was waiting for her upstairs, this time I reached before the scheduled time so I had to wait for her. She reached after half an hour. She was in her school dress of a white shirt and blue skirt, her hair tied in a neat manner. This was the first time that I saw her in the school dress and she was looking so cute like a kid that I couldn't resist myself from laughing. As soon as she reached upstairs, she patted me and said "*Kyu has raha hai, pitega kya?*" and she also started laughing.

I hugged her tightly without noticing anything around us because I knew it was only she who could make me happy and help me to come out of this devastating situation. A single hug from her gave me a sense of relief that she was with me and she was there to take care of me always. Her presence in my life was just like a medicine for a disease which is incurable. She was the reason for my smile; her innocence melted my sadness and gave me strength to live happily. We met at Kohat multiple times in the month of September. She used to come to meet me after her school. If her friends asked her why she always got down at Kohat, she always had a different excuse every time. Every meeting with her made me realize how lucky I was, as she always cared for me; she always wanted me to be happy and she always tried to make the relationship her priority.

With the passage of time everything settled down as after all, time heals everything.

25th September, 2009 (First Kiss)

After convincing my Mamaji after a lot of coaxing and begging, this was the day when he agreed to get me a new bike. We went to the showroom and searched for a bike which would fit my budget. I wanted a sports bike but it was out of my budget and Mamaji suggested that I get a Hero Honda Glamour. I did not have any choice but I had to agree. After all, having a bike will help me to meet Megha more frequently and to reach on time. I always had a dream to take her for a bike ride.

I got my new bike home and the very next day I went outside her house to show her my new bike. She was not excited as she didn't like riding bikes; she was afraid what if her relatives saw us together on a bike, and I understand how difficult it is for a girl to save herself from the talk of relatives. Though my dream of a bike ride with her broke, I reminded myself that in her happiness lies my happiness. The purpose for buying a bike was served, as now I started meeting her very frequently which had not been possible earlier as I had to hire a rickshaw every time and it took a lot of time to reach the destination.

It was somewhere in November, as I said before I am bad at remembering the dates; we met in the park. I wanted to kiss her, and she was afraid to do so, as she thought that kissing a guy can make a woman pregnant. Hearing this I laughed a lot, but this was not a big thing to laugh at, as in some schools teachers still restrain themselves from giving proper biology education to the students. I explained her that kissing doesn't make a woman pregnant, though it was difficult for her to trust but she trusted me blindly.

I had never kissed any one till then, and neither had she. We both were new at it; both were nervous and confused about how to kiss. "First of all," I said to her, "Let's find a place where nobody could see us,". We saw a truck which was parked outside the main gate of the park. We went behind that truck and confirmed that no one would be able to see us there. I was so nervous that I couldn't understand that whether I should start first or should she? But the instinct of male dominance inside me told me that a guy always starts. She said nothing and just stood still and calm before me. I put my left hand on her waist which she didn't resist, and I pulled her towards me. I locked my right hand with her right hand tightly. Slowly we started coming very close each other, she was breathing heavily and I could feel her warm breath. We both kissed each other and I could feel her soft rosy lips moving in between my lips. I felt complete after this.

This was the day when our souls met each other. We both smiled and through her eyes she asked me to leave her waist.

She was getting late as she had told her mom that she had to buy something from the market and would be back within 15 minutes. We both did not wanted to leave so early as we both were feeling high, but we had too.

When I came back home I called her and asked her, "How was it??"

She smiled and answered, "It's a completely different feeling, and I feel complete after this,"

"I want to kiss you again, I did not wanted to leave so early but you had to go. I love you," I said.

"I Love you too," she replied.

We both couldn't sleep that night. After every few minutes we kept calling each other, we both had nothing to say during the phone call, the only thing which we did was call each other and smile. We both enjoyed the silence of the night flashing back to the kissing scene again and again.

In December 2009 though she was preparing for her 12th board exams, we continued to meet each other several times. Sometimes we had small fights between us on minor issues but still it was an awesome relationship. She never got angry and always accepted me for what I am.

23rd January, 2010 (My First Birthday with her)

12:00 am, my phone rang and as I was waiting for her, the first caller.

"Happy birthday sweetheart," she said.

"Thank you,"

"Love you sweetheart,"

"Love you to,"

"Listen, Kavya wants to talk to you,"

"Okay,"

"Happy Birthday," this was Kavya from the other side.

"Thank you,"

"I want you to meet me at Rohini East Metro station at 9 am,"

"Why?"

"That's a surprise. Good night,"

"Good night,"

08:00 am, again it's the call from Megha.

"Good morning. Happy birthday…"

"Good morning, thank you!"

"Remember? You have to meet Kavya at Rohini East at 9…"

"Yes, I am getting ready and will reach on time,"

I was wondering what the surprise could be, I reached Rohini East at 9 and waited for Kavya to come. She came and after wising me 'Happy birthday!' she gave me a packet and said to me 'Here, it's your gift,", she has to go to college after that so she left in a hurry.

I opened the packet; it was a brown color shirt and a birthday card. She knew very well that I did not have a brown colored shirt and I look good in brown color. I liked the shirt and tried to wear it, but damn it! It was large size shirt and I wear small size shirts. I thought if I would have been able to wear it she would be happy but I couldn't.

Yes, I too wondered why Megha sent me this gift through Kavya and why she herself did not gave it to me.

11:00 am, me and Megha had planned to celebrate my birthday at Pizza Hut in Metro Walk (Rohini), so we reached there. I was still wondering, what was the reason behind sending that gift through Kavya and I finally asked her the reason behind this.

She said, I don't have a car and if I would have taken the shirt at my home then my mom would have asked me about it. So I left the shirt in Kavya's car and asked her to give it to you. Why didn't you wear that shirt today?

I was feeling very indifferent and confused about what to answer. But I did not want to hide anything from her so I said, it was large size and I wear small size shirts.

Oh! Just get it altered and next time wear it; I haven't seen that shirt yet as Kavya bought it for you. You know na, due to exams I am barely allowed to go out of home,"

"I understand sweet heart..."

"Order Sir???" the Pizza Hut boy popped up in between.

I have never been to Pizza Hut before and did I knew how to see a menu. I was a small town boy after all.

"One 'Veggie Lover's Pizza' medium, one 'Garlic Bread', and two lemonades for us please..." she said.

She ordered in such a way that she was very frequent at all these restaurants. She smiled and asked me "Anything else you would like?"

No, it's enough I guess. "I mean anything else?? I dint even knew what she had ordered till now, I do not have any idea,"

But she knew it that I have never been to any Pizza Hut type restaurant and she made me learn how to look at a menu.

"Oh! It's so simple. I never knew it," I said smiling.

"Hmm, next time you will order," she said.

The pizza arrived and we both had our lunch.

"How was the Pizza?" she asked me.

"It was awesome, just like you; after all it was your choice," I said.

"To tease me she said, you are also my choice, but you are not that awesome." and smiled mischievously.

Now it was the time for her to go home and as usual I felt very bad about it, as I never wanted her to go away from me and I wanted her to be with me forever. But we had to depart and I was happy to spend my time with her, after all she was everything for me now.

February 2010 (Simran Kaur)

I had my exams for B.Com 2nd year in the month of June so I had to join the crash course classes for subjects like Tax and Mathematics. Again it was the first day of the same institute NGPA. A few faces were the same but many of them were new to the institute. Then I saw the same girl who never used to talk to me and always used to sit on the back bench, Simran Kaur.

She came to me and asked me if she could sit on the chair to my left side. I had no problem and she was comfortable sitting next to me. I was more confident in the classes now. I had nothing to feel nervous about because I had learned to behave well and maintain myself.

Slowly we became friends and exchanged numbers too. Sometimes she used to message me to ask about the classes, or the schedules but very soon because of frequent chats through messages we became good friends and then we always used to sit next to each other in the classes. She was beautiful and of course she was good at heart.

The Mathematics classes were very boring for both of us; as none of us had any interest in Math's, so often we used to play "Zero Kata" on the note books. Two, three times our teacher caught us playing and ordered us to sit apart from each other. But who cared, we always used to sit together, after all we were the disturbing elements in the class.

Megha knew everything about me and my friendship with Simran and how we disturbed the whole class, but she never had any problem with this, as she always trusted me blindly and she knew that I'll always **Love** her and never ever cheat on her.

One day Simran asked me to come half an hour before the class; I wondered what was going on in her mind. I reached the institute and asked her for the reason behind calling me so early. She said she wanted to spend some time with me, and I was confused how to behave. I thought maybe she was sad and she considered me a good friend that's why she wanted to spend some time with me. So I was okay with it.

The next day she did the same but I couldn't reach before the class. We attended the class and after the class I asked her the reason behind calling me half hour before the class every day, but she dint replied and left for the home.

As soon as I reached home I got a call from her.

"Hey!"

"Hello, did you reach home safely?" she asked.

"Yes, I did. My home is just a kilometer away from the institute, did you reach home?"

"No, I am on the way; I am in the bus right now,"

"Okay,"

Then I asked her about the purpose behind calling me before the class every day, she said she just wanted to spend some time with me alone. I was feeling very indifferent, I mean I dint know what was going on with her and I was very surprised from her behavior towards me. I asked her whether everything was okay at her home. She said everything was alright but still she was feeling very alone. I told her that I could not come before the class timings every day and if she was feeling sad about something or if she had some problem she could share it with me and then I'll try to solve it. She said she was also confused about what was going on in her mind and she would try to figure it out.

In the evening she called me and said she that she was Love with me. That is why she wanted to spend time with me, that is the reason behind calling me after the class and asking me whether I had reached home or had my food on time or not.

I had mixed emotions now, on the one hand I was happy that after meeting Megha. I had improved so much that the girl who never even talked to me a year ago had now proposed me, but on the other hand I was worried about what Megha would feel listening to this - that I had been proposed to by another girl. I never hide anything from Megha and I had to first tell Simran that I was committed and I couldn't say yes to her. I knew that I was going to break her heart but I had no choice and I had too.

I tried to convince Simran that I was already committed to someone for the last one year and I couldn't cheat on her for anyone in this entire world. I told her that I always considered her as a good friend of mine and I did not have any feelings for her. Listening to this she cried a lot and disconnected the call, and I knew may be she will not talk to me ever after this.

I was more worried about Megha, I called her and explained her everything. I thought Megha was going to shout at me and would get angry with me, but she was not. She said few words "I know you are mine, and I know you will always be.". This narrates the whole story of her trust in me. These few words of her melted me and made me love her more.

The next day Simran Kaur was behaving as usual and she had convinced herself that I am committed and we can be good friends always. Sometimes she used to become a bit sad because I dint accept her proposal but she was a fun loving girl so she always convinced herself that she deserves someone else and we were good friends again.

The First Fight

After her board exams for the 12th Standard, Megha started taking classes for her BBA entrance exams in an institute. Sakshi and her friends also joined the same institute for their BBA entrance preparation. One day Megha called me to ask me whether I could meet her outside the Movie Time cinema hall, she said Sakshi was going to meet Lalit (her boyfriend) so we can also meet at the same place as she either way she had to go along with Sakshi. I agreed and went to the pre-decided place, Lalit and I were waiting for our girlfriends and then they came. We unlike others used to meet in the stairs of the Movie hall as no one was there to disturb us. It was a bit awkward for me but Megha had called me to meet her, so I had to adjust myself to sit on the stairs and spend time with Megha, till the meeting of Sakshi and Lalit finished. I never wanted to meet her like this but Megha had to go with Sakshi and she would have got very bored if I had not joined her there.

Whenever Sakshi had to meet Lalit, she always used to tell her mom that she was going for the class and her mom knew that Sakshi and Megha were in the same class. So when Sakshi was meeting Lalit, Megha couldn't be at home. Sakshi and Lalit started meeting frequently and Megha had to go along with Sakshi. Sometimes the plans to meet were made so quickly that I had to go leaving everything I was doing unfinished. This started building frustration in my mind, as I didn't wanted Megha to go along with Sakshi just to get bored and I also at the same time I did not want to meet her like this. Many times we had a lot of small fights between us on this issue but somehow we both managed to keep each other happy.

On her 2nd birthday with me I wanted to gift her something different so I asked her what she would like to get as a gift for her birthday. She said she would love if someone sent her a bouquet at her home at the stroke of midnight. Though her family is strict on these things on birthdays they say nothing.

I said her that I am never going to do it as maybe her family would ask her who had sent her the flowers and they might doubt Megha and suspect that she has a boyfriend. I said this to her because I wanted Megha to not to expect the bouquet in the night as I would have not been able to surprise her with the bouquet.

A day before her birthday I went to the florist near her house and asked him to send the best bouquet he had to Megha at midnight. With the flowers I sent a card which contained the name of the sender. The florist wanted me to write the sender's name but I wrote "From all your Friends". The florist sent the bouquet to her in the night and she was very surprised to get it as she never expected it. I called her to wish her happy birthday and she thanked me for the bouquet.

One day I asked Megha to meet me at the Movie Time hall, she came to meet me bunking her classes, this time we met alone and after having spent some time with each other she got a call from her Grandmother. Her Grandmother thought that Megha was in the class, but she was with me. Her grandmother said "Megha I am coming towards your institute as I have some work in the nearby market. By the time I am done with the work your class will be over so you can come home with me,"

Megha got very worried and she now had to reach her institute somehow. I asked her to board an auto, but she said she would not be able to reach their quickly and what if her Grandmother saw her sitting inside the auto while going towards her institute. Then I asked her to sit on my bike and I would drop her to the institute. She had no choice, so she had to go with me. This was the first time when she was riding on my bike and I had to drop her to the institute as quickly as possible. From the movie hall where we met, her home was on the way to her institute, so I had to take a different route to reach her institute, but that route was blocked. So I had to take a reverse and I said "Megha, either we will reach your institute before you Grandmother reaches or someone is going to see us together, because your house is on the way to your institute, so get ready to face the consequences if anyone from your family sees us together,"

This was the first dare which we both did together and I drove my bike as fast as I could towards her institute.

Though we both were very afraid of getting caught by her family members, we reached the institute on time and nobody could see us together. This was the first time when she praised my bike driving and it was a completely adventurous ride which we had together that day. Sometimes while driving towards the market I still miss that day.

After her exams in June, because of not getting selected in good college for BBA, she got admission in Laxmibai College with was affiliated to Delhi University. She started doing her BA from there, she has to go to her college by auto and it took a lot of time to reach there so soon she got her first car. She learned driving during her BBA entrance exam preparations and I was a bit jealous that she knew how to drive a car and I didn't.

She was fond of trying new dishes and visiting new places, just as I was. I love to eat but I am very choosy. Sometimes when we went to the restaurants, she was okay with anything which I ordered in the restaurant but I had few choices and I sometimes did not like the food which she ordered, so many times we ordered different things for both of us. In the month of August she took me to a place where she used to eat "Corn Chat", she wanted me to try it as I had never tried it. I tried the "Corn Chat" and liked it too. After having it we both went inside her car, we were love birds and I always wanted to park her car in a place where no one can see us sitting inside the car, it was because of two reasons. One, her relatives are everywhere in Delhi as she said. Two, I wanted a kiss before going away from her. So as I insisted she drove her car through many roads to find a suitable place to park the car and she hated driving because of the traffic. She used to shout at me for this "Is it necessary to park a car and have a chat with me?" and always my answer used to be "While driving you cannot pay attention to me, while driving I cannot see you properly. I want to see your eyes while talking to you; I want to get lost in your beauty, I want you to see my expression while I am talking to you, I want to kiss you before you leave me alone for the next few days and she used to smile and always find a place where we could park the car, talk to each other, hug each other and kiss each other before leaving.

But that day was different, she found a place to park the car and we started talking to each other. I don't know from where it came, the topic of a guy started. Actually she was talking to an unknown guy on Yahoo messenger the last few days and I knew about it and I have read all the chats between them because we both ensured that we had transparency in our relationship. We knew each other's ids and passwords. That guy sent her the request to add her and she accepted it. I told her that every guy is same in case of a girl, but she said every guy is not the same. She said I am talking to him just as a friend and

I knew that she was talking to him just as a friend; but being a man I couldn't see her talking to an unknown guy. I had an objection to her chats with that guy but she said that I was also unknown to her once, and that she said she knows her limits and when the guy is going to cross his limits she would not talk to him. I said just wait for few days, he is going to propose you and she said that it was not going to happen. Guess what? The guy tried to show her that he was in love with her and he showed that he became unwell when Megha didn't talk to him, I mean really?? Does it happen?? It happens only when we are in a relationship, not in a friendship. I told Megha to block that person and not to talk to him after this. She blocked him and I said "See all guys are same in case of a girl!" She again disagreed to this and said that they aren't. I got angry with this and I said you are behaving just like a characterless woman that would talk to anybody on the street and share anything. I knew I was wrong and out of my limits, as Megha had already stopped talking to him and she was doing everything according to me. "The biggest crime is to blame someone who is truly innocent." and I committed this crime for which she was very angry with me for several days. She didn't talk to me for two, three days and I had to say sorry to her for that.

Now while sitting inside the car she pulled out the topic of me blaming her for being a characterless woman, I said to her that I had already apologized for it and I would never repeat it again but when a girl starts an argument on something you never know when it is going to end. She then said something which a guy would never like to hear, she said "If I am characterless, every girl in your family is characterless!". This worked as a catalyst for making me angry. I couldn't digest her blame and I slapped her for this.

"A real man never slaps his women; he is always expected to love her, as a girl always sacrifices everything for her man."

I was full of guilt and I realized that I am from a family where my father never did this to my mom, how can I do this with Megha. She started crying and said "My father also gets angry with my mom, but he never slaps her." I apologized to her for this and I promised I would never do it again, but she was so hurt that she did not want to talk to me after this.

I went home, locked myself inside a room, slapped myself and cried a lot. Not only had I disrespected myself in front of her, I also lost respect for myself. This was the worst mistake of my life which I never wanted to do but while I am angry I never realize my words and actions. Someone had truly said "Never promise anything when you are very happy and never take any decision when you are very angry about something."

I tried to call her several times but she did not receive the call, I messaged her but she did not reply. I called Kavya to ask her to pick up my call but even then she did not pick up my call. I was damn worried, broken, frustrated, hurt and tense about this mistake. I never wanted to lose her, she was my life and she meant everything to me.

I realized this time that I loved her more then I loved anyone else in this world, and I considered Love as being next to god. The next day I called her and she said she didn't want to talk to me anymore. I tried to convince her but she disconnected the call. On the third day I again tried to convince her that I didn't realize what I had done in anger and I am ready to accept any punishment that she wanted to give me for this. She made me promise that I would accept any punishment which she gave me for this. She said I would have to touch her feet and say sorry for this mistake and I also had to promise not to repeat this mistake ever.

"*When a women touches a man's feet it's okay, so why can't a man do the same?*". *Then I had two choices with me now "Either I can let go of my male ego - win and lose my love forever, or be man enough to touch her feet and say sorry and be with her forever*". I accepted her punishment and I touched her feet the next day when we met. She was happy that I dropped my ego and was man enough to realize my mistake and I had done something which someone else would have never done to get her back. She hugged me for this and we were happy once again.

The Dreamer's Fantasy Come True

September 2010

Like any other couple we both used to talk over the phone till late at night. Sometimes we used to talk till early morning. One September night, we were talking to each other on the phone and it started raining outside. I could hear the sound of raindrops falling on the sheds of my flat and I went to the balcony to see the rain.
I said "Megha, it's raining outside, do you love rain?"

She smiled and replied "Yes I do,"

I, being a bit pessimistic said that I didn't like rain because it creates traffic and causes bike tires to slip while driving. You cannot go out of home neatly dressed as it creates a lot of problem while walking on the roads. She on the other hand being an optimist said she loved to walk in the rain, and that she wanted to dance with me in the rain.

But the rain also induced a romantic feeling in the both of us. God had given us all the gift of imagination, so that whenever we read or listen to something, we start visualizing it. We both started to visualize our honeymoon after our marriage. We were going towards the hotel in a hilly area with an empty road, surrounded by green trees on both the sides. I was driving the car in the pitch black night; she was sitting next to me. She is dressed in complete white and me in a black suit, we both were alone and no one was there to see us. Suddenly it starts raining and I stop the car, we both smiled looking at each other and got out of the car leaving the headlights on. We played her favorite song "*Pehla nasha, pehla khumaar, naya pyar hai, naya intazaar....*" I held her right hand with my left hand and kept my right hand on her waist, her left hand was on my right shoulder and we started dancing. I could clearly see the raindrops falling on her eyebrows and then slowly falling down to her cheeks and then on her soft rosy lips; she was looking towards me and I knew she is feeling shy but I couldn't stop myself from looking at her wet, glossy lips. I went close to her, by then the music stopped and there was complete silence, so I went ahead and kissed her. I could feel her so close that I just wanted to be there for few more minutes, but she was shivering because of the cold or may be because of her nervousness. As a gentleman would, I opened my jacket and gave it to her. We both went back inside the car and drove toward the hotel.

Suddenly the rain stopped and both of us snapped out of our dream with our open eyes.

"Would you always love me like this?" she asked.

"Yes I will," I replied.

"Promise??"

"Promise!"

"*Achha*, what after we went inside the room of the hotel...what happened then..." I asked her.

She was feeling shy, she said to me coyly "You tell..."

"Umm... We both have reached inside the room, I locked the door from inside, you started walking towards the bathroom to change your dress but there was no light in the room so you stayed in the room itself. We searched for the candles and lit them. I asked you to change the clothes in the room itself if you felt comfortable. You smiled and said "*Ok but you will not look at me till I change my clothes.*". I said okay and you turned your back to me, you started taking out your earrings and then your white gown, I was looking at your wet back and you somehow came to know that I am looking at you, but you did not react as you knew that your mine now and you don't have any problem with me looking at you. Now you started taking the gown off your legs. You left the gown on the bed and I could see you wrapping your hair with the towel. I started coming close to you...and I touched your shoulders and..."

"And..." she asked.

"And the lights are on and you have to change your clothes sweetheart!" I laughed mischievously.

She also started laughing with me...

We made up a plan to meet at my home next day, my Mamaji and Mami had to leave to attend a marriage in Rajasthan and Ravi has to go to the office.

In the morning I woke up early to see that the plan to meet Megha was in working order. I saw Mamaji and Mami getting ready to go to the marriage and soon they were off. Mamaji told me to take care of the house and they left. Now it was Ravi who had to leave, I woke him up and told him that it was 10 am and he had to leave for his office. Ravi woke up shouting "Shit I am getting late!"

and hurried towards the bathroom. I was feeling very happy and I smiled thinking that the plan was working out perfectly. Soon Ravi took his breakfast and left for the office. I got ready now and was waiting for Megha to come. She called me and said the guards were asking me which house number you are going into, and they wanted her to make an entry in the register. I asked her to enter a fake name and fake number in the register. She did so and came to my house. Before letting her in I ensured that no one was looking towards the door and I took her inside, and locked the door.

Now it was me and her, all alone, total silence. She was looking stunning in her black top and blue jeans. We both went towards my room, I showed her my almirah, my laptop and the note book in which I used to write the poems. Now we both were sitting next to each other and smiling. I wanted to kiss her; I held her hand and kissed it. She smiled and pulled a pillow to put it on her lap. I laid my head on that pillow and told her that I had been waiting for such moment when I put my head on her lap and she put her hand on my head and slowly raked her fingers across my hair. She did the same and then I kissed her on her head.

I slowly went close to her now and hugged her, she was breathing slowly and I could hear her whispering **"I Love You!"** in my ear, I replied **"I Love you too!"**. I adjusted the curtains of my room to prevent the light from coming inside. I then kissed her on her lips; I could feel her warm breath while kissing, and we both were lost in each other now. We kept on kissing each other. Looking at her I smiled and I started with a kiss on her head - a kiss of love, then a kiss on her eyes - a kiss of care, then a kiss on her cheeks - a kiss of affection, then a kiss on her nose, a kiss of trust, then a kiss on her lips - a kiss of romance and then finally a kiss on her neck, a kiss of seduction. We both were now the world of each other. I could feel her smell and it was mesmerizing me. Every lady has a different smell, and that smell makes a man go down on his knees to get that women. I then kissed each and every cell of her. We both were now totally on each other's hands and that was the most romantic day of our intimate relationship.

After few hours which we spent together she had to go home. She dressed up and started walking towards the main gate, I held her hand and pulled her towards me and again we both were silently standing in front of each other, I kissed her again and then she left. I was feeling very different now as I had given myself to her forever. I called her and said "After everything which we had today I am totally yours, and I will always be," She was very happy to listen to this and replied "I am very happy to have you in my life; I promise I'll always be yours and yours only!" This was the happiest day of my life.

But you never know what the time and fate has decided for us, "*Whenever I am very happy, something bad happens*". A month after this we were caught by the police kissing each other in a car. The policeman asked me to come out and threatened me by saying that he would take both of us to the police station and call our families and tell them what we were doing. We were very afraid but suddenly I got an idea 'Money makes the mayor go!' is the famous adage". I bribed the policeman. This solved our problem and we were free to go from there.

After that Megha was very introverted; she never wanted people to know about us. But my life on the other hand was an open book for everybody to read and except for a few very serious things I never hid anything from anyone in my family. Megha got angry and hurt thinking about that incident and she asked me not to meet her in the car like this. I agreed because I always wanted to keep her happy. We started meeting each other in the nearby malls and parks then.

23rd January, 2011 (My Birthday)

My cousin Preeti was in Delhi, in 2011 for her CS exams preparation. Megha already knew all of my cousins so I asked her if she didn't mind me taking Ravi and Preeti along with us to celebrate my birthday. She was okay with it and we all planned to go to Rajaouri Garden for my birthday party. Rajaouri Garden is a nice place to do some shopping, and I personally like that place because I find it quite calm and beautiful.

Megha was waiting for all of us at the Kohat Metro Station in her car. Me, Preeti and Ravi came to Kohat on the metro and then we had to go to Rajaouri in Megha's Car. Of course me and Megha were a couple so as she was driving I had to sit in the front seat of the car on her left side and Ravi and Preeti adjusted themselves on the backseat. Megha and me had a habit of changing the FM Stations while we are inside the car; sometimes I didn't like the songs which she played and sometimes she didn't liked what I played, but it was a sweet and sour type competition between us - who could change the maximum number of stations!

Finally we reached Rajaouri; we barely knew what all restaurants were there so we didn't know where we could have our lunch. I asked all of them what they would like to have, though they had only two options. One is to have a proper lunch in a restaurant which includes food like "Naan, mixed vegetable korma and daal makhni" or the other option is to have a pizza party. As usual Megha said "I would have anything, I don't have any problem!" Preeti, Ravi and I were pizza lovers. So we found the restaurant named Papa John's Pizza, which was new to all of us, as none of us had ever been there. We all settled in a table for four people. As usual I handed over the menu to my sweetheart to order as she knows what I liked. She asked Preeti and Ravi about their choices and ordered the pizzas. I was a bit confused about the taste of the pizzas in that restaurant as I had never been to any pizza restaurant except Pizza Hut and Dominos. But the pizzas were good and we all liked them.

After the pizza party now we had to go home, so we left the restaurant and were walking towards the basement where the car was parked. I was feeling very awkward while walking towards the basement, as I wanted to hug Megha but Preeti and Ravi were there so I couldn't. I was just thinking of any excuse with which Megha and I could be alone for some time. I got many ideas through which I could be alone with Megha for a while, it was my birthday after all and I wanted to hug my girl and feel happy but then I thought that I would send Preeti and Ravi home when we reach Kohat and ill stay with Megha in the car for a while. I would be able to spend some time alone with my Love.

Now we reached the car, and I was wondering how come none of them had bought any gift for me. I was expecting a gift from all of them, I was like a kid in that sense – I loved getting gifts on my birthday. Megha opened the front door of the car and took out a birthday card and gave it to me. It was a long card which had 12 small cards in it, each card having a different message. While looking at the messages on the card I opened the door of car and was about to sit inside, but Megha and Preeti called me towards the back of the car. I went there and saw that there was a cake inside the back of the car. Megha and Preeti both smiled at me and said "*Tujhe kya laga koi gift nahi laya tere liye*?"

Megha had brought this cake for me; she opened the box of the cake and said "It's your favorite chocolate cake!"

Preeti and Ravi helped Megha in lighting the candles and then they all started singing the song "Happy birthday to you, Happy birthday to you…" I was given a knife to cut the cake; I know it was going to sound surprising but this was the first time that I was actually going to cut a cake on my birthday. Megha held my hand and helped me to cut it. Whenever I used to eat anything I always asked Megha to bite it first, according to me this increases the taste of the food, similarly the first sip of any liquid I used to have, went to her. So when I cut the cake the first bite was tasted by her, and that increased the taste of my favorite chocolate cake. I remember the day when Megha asked me about my favorite cake and I said I had never cut a cake in my life till date but my favorite cake was chocolate cake. She knew that she would make this birthday special by bringing a cake for me and making me do something which I had never done in last 20 years. Eventually this day became the happiest day of my life as

I was with such a girl. A girl who always wanted to make me happy by doing beautiful things for me.

After having the cake we all were now inside the car and then Preeti asked me not to touch the FM this time, she said Megha plays the right song. "All girls are same!" I said and Ravi and I burst out into laughter. Soon we reached Kohat and I asked Ravi to take Preeti home and informed him that I would spend some time with Megha and would be back at home soon. They understood my feelings left us alone, and now I was with Megha in her car.

She asked me "How was the cake *Jaan*?"

I said "It was not tastier than you sweetheart,"

She smiled and asked me "Did you enjoy your birthday with us today?".

"Yes, but I need one more gift from you."

She asked "What do you want sweet heart?"

I asked her to put her hand on my head and take an oath that she would never leave me and would always love me like this. She smiled and did the same. She was a perfect girl who would do anything for her boyfriend's happiness. As I had wanted to from the moment I had seen her earlier that day, I hugged her and kissed her.

Sadly, the moment when I had to go home came very soon I said, "*Yaar tujhse door jaane me na Jaan si nikal jaati hai, kash mai hamesha tere sath reh sakta, shaadi kar le tu mujhse abhi.*"

She smiled and said she is only 17 yet and is not allowed to marry according to law. The Law was "*Kabab me haddi* this time", I mean I had no words after this reply.

"Okay see ya sweetheart, enjoy your birthday, happy birthday once again!" she said

"Thank you, **I Love You**..."

"**Love you** too..." she replied

"See ya".

28th May, 2011

It was her third birthday with me when we went to D Mall, Netaji Subhash Palace. But on that special day of hers we were unable to plan a proper celebration just like we had done for our birthdays together earlier due to some family problem in her house. So we planned to have a small birthday party just at Haldiram's at the D Mall. I waited for her at Kohat Enclave Metro station, as usual she was late but it was her birthday so I decided not to get angry with her. She came after few minutes, I went near her car and she opened the door lock. As soon as I entered inside the car she smiled and all my anger went away. Her smile was one thing which could melt all of my anger.

"Are you angry with me?" she asked.

"I was but your smile took away all of my anger and gave me a reason to Love you again sweet heart..."

She smiled and I hugged her. She was looking very beautiful that day; I noticed she was in her favorite pink top and white designed long skirt. She was looking prettier than ever and I complimented her and she said impishly that she always looked pretty and I had to agree with her. After all she always looked more beautiful than ever. We reached D Mall in a few minutes but we both were not feeling hungry at all so we decided to sit on the stairs. Actually those stairs are not allowed to be used except in case of emergency, but as we were love birds we had to make a nest in a prohibited place to make sure that we were alone and no one disturbed us.

She was sitting on the top most stairs and I was on the second one. We were sitting hand in hand and were talking about our families and then suddenly she became a bit sad thinking of her family problem. I knew how to cheer her up.

I said "Never feel sad about anything, as whatever is happening is happening because we do not have control over it, and if you are sad who will take care of the whole family, if you are sad then my happiness will go away; just look at me and smile, I am always with you,"

She knew that when she was sad I also become sad, so she smiled and said "I know you are always there for me, when you are there I feel safe and confident enough to fight all the problems in the world!"

To divert her mood I started clicking her pictures on my new phone and she started giving me seductive poses like a celebrity. This time I did not have any gift for her as she did not tell anyone at her home that she was going out to celebrate her birthday. I wanted to give her few gifts but I had to take care of her feelings and I decided to make her next birthday better than ever.

June 2011 (One more proposal)

I was in my home town on vacation and as usual I was going through my FB profile; I saw a friend request from one of my class mates from 12th, Jyoti. She was the most studious and intelligent girl in our class, I remembered though I was also studious and always in the top five of the class we used to help each other a lot in studies. But except for the studies we did not have any conversation and had not been good friends. I accepted the request and like any other old school classmate she was now my FB friend. A normal conversation between us led to the sharing of phone numbers, and now we started chatting over the text messages instead of on Facebook.

I asked her whether she was in contact with any of our other classmates. She replied that she was in contact with a few of them. She was completely different from what I had thought of her, according to me she was a reserved kind of girl who never shared anything until someone asked her directly but here she was an extrovert and she clearly had the urge to share lots of information with people. She told me how one of her cousins ran away from home with her boyfriend and their family found her, brought her back and got her married to some other guy. The reason behind it was simple; that the people in villages are orthodox, and the girl and boy were from different religions, so they did not accept the relationship.

She then wanted to know about me, whether I had a girl friend or not. I told her about Megha. Then she told me about Apoorva, another classmate of ours who liked me and wanted to talk to me, but I had never talked to her as I never liked her. Then I asked her whether she has a boyfriend, she said she likes a boy but he was from different religion so her parents would not allow her to marry him. She said she wanted to stop talking to him and that is why she changed her number, but she was not able to forget him.

Meanwhile I got message from an unknown number, and it was Apoorva who seemed to have taken my number from Jyoti. Now this was a complete mess for me as I never wanted many people to enter my life and disturb me, as I am a person who has always had limited friends. I don't believe in making too many friends. I never liked this girl Apoorva and I did not wanted to talk to her, so I bluntly asked her to stop messaging me.

With the passage of a few days Jyoti too got inclined towards me, she said she wants to forget her boyfriend and if I allow she would like to be my girlfriend. I was like 'What the hell is going on? She knows that I am already committed to someone and still she has the guts to propose me this way!' I reminded her that I was in a relationship for the last two years and that I love Megha very much. I tried to figure it out but I failed to analyze what was going on in Jyoti's head. She remained in contact with me for few more months after that but it was just as a friend and I too ensured that I did not talk to her much.

I explained everything to Megha and I was expecting her to get angry. But surprise, she was not at all angry with me. She said "See how lucky I am. When I am in your life a lot of girls are proposing you, and with the rejection of this proposal we have come closer than ever. Now I am more confident that you will always be mine!"

I smiled and said "Sweet heart you are completely unpredictable; you trust me so much that I could never even think of breaking your heart. I'll always be yours and will never go away from you…"

This was the way in which she was completely different from others, unlike other girls she is not angry and her trust is stronger than her insecurity, but I was completely different, I felt insecure even when she talked to another guy, but this doesn't mean that I don't trust her, I did. But like other guys out there I had a sense of insecurity and I always wanted her to talk only to good friends. We always remained reserved from other and stuck to each other. So much so that we never used to interact with other people much and we used to spend all of our spare time with each other or on the phone talking to each other.

July 2011 (B – School)

My B.Com final year exams were over and now I had to do my postgraduate studies. Megha wanted me to stop studying and start doing business as she thought that instead of studying for the next two years if I started doing business, I would be able to buy my own house, and I will be able to create enough goodwill to ask for her hand in those two years. According to her, her father would only allow me to marry her when I had a good business and my own house in Delhi. This made sense as of course every father would like to get his daughter married to a well-settled guy. She was right on her part as she wanted to marry me and she wanted me to become something in my life. But because it was my dream to become an MBA, I promised her that after post-graduation that I would surely start my own business and would buy my own house in Delhi. She let me do so and she was happy for me.

I had always wanted to become an MBA but my relatives suggested that I should do either CA or CS instead of MBA. My family members always wanted me to become a CA, but as I was very weak in Math, I never wanted to go for a postgraduate program which I could not complete. CS was also a good option but I knew if I opted for CS then I would not be able to enjoy college life and to become an MBA was my dream since childhood days. The decision to do an MBA was finalized but due to my poor marks in my B.Com I could not do CAT and MAT exams which led me to search for some private institute to do my MBA from.

I started searching on internet about the top private colleges and I came across the website of IIPM (Indian Institute of Planning and Management), in 2011, IIPM was ranked the fifth-best business school in India in the Zee Best Business School survey results. In the same survey it was ranked first in India in terms of Global Exposure and intellectual impact, fifth in terms of course contents and overall placements, third in industry interface and sixteenth on infrastructural facilities. At the 2011 Asia's Best B-School awards ceremony, IIPM was judged the 2011 Best B-school in Asia Overall. In DNA's 2011 National B-School Survey, IIPM was ranked eighth-best B-school in India. In the same survey, IIPM was ranked first in international exposure, eleventh in curriculum, ninth in intellectual impact, sixth in image of the institute, eleventh in placements, sixth in industry interaction, eighth in infrastructure and twelfth in potential to network. In the 2011 B-School Survey of *Mail Today*, IIPM was ranked top of all B-schools surveyed.

I was very excited to get admission in IIPM now. I jumped up to the 'Contact Us' page and filled up the credentials; soon I got a call for an interview and a written test for admission. Though I had never given any interview in the past I passed both the written test and the oral interview. They now asked me to choose the campus, and I opted for the Delhi campus. I got very excited when they sent me the selection letter when my admission was confirmed.

August 2011

IIPM called the new students to the Orientation Program in Sri Satya Sai Auditorium on Lodhi Road. The dress code was 'Formals' and I had never worn any formals in my life before that. I borrowed the formals from my cousin and I was very excited to go to the Orientation Program. I reached the auditorium at the exact time given in the invitation letter. I was a bit nervous to see so many new people and I didn't know any one of them. Everyone was well dressed and behaved in a very sophisticated manner. Soon we entered the auditorium and it was filled up like a movie theater. Mr. Arindham Chaudhary gave a very motivational speech along with his wife Mrs. Rajita Chaudhary and then they announced the date of our first class at IIPM.

30th August, 2011

It was the first day of my college. I boarded the bus organized by IIPM from Netaji Subhash Palace. I thought I would be the only one to board the bus from NSP but I wasn't. Soon a girl entered the bus, wearing a black top, blue denim and a purple jacket having a black purse in her hand. She was slim and beautiful, she came and sat behind me and said bye to her daddy who was sitting in a black BMW. Then entered another girl, a bit healthy not to be confused with fat, she had messy hair which was curly from the top and straight at the bottom, a square face with red lipstick. She was wearing a red top and black jeans, carrying a pink colored bag in her hand. She was wearing a pair of high heeled sandals as she was only 5feet tall. She sat on the right side seat to me and said bye to her daddy who has come to drop her. The journey to college was one and half hour from there and all of us were strangers so we kept quiet during the whole journey.

We reached the college at 8:15am and the class was about to start at 8:30am, I searched the classroom and made myself comfortable in the front seat as all of the backseats were occupied till I reached the class. When I glanced at all the faces in the class I came to know that the two girls who came in the same bus with me were my classmates. The 'Girl with the BMW Daddy' (as I had referred to her) was Sahiba Wadhwa and the 'Girl wearing High Heels' was Simran Chawla. The classroom was completely filled up, and everyone was busy introducing themselves to each other. A guy sitting on my right introduced himself to me, "Hi! My Name is Iman Roy." He was a Bengali and his accent revealed this. I then introduced myself, "Hi! I am Chandra Kant,"

I was surprised to see that on the first day everyone was speaking in very good English and I have never been so fluent but somehow I managed to communicate with everyone. Soon the Professor of Accounts Mr. Alok Khanna entered the class; he was 6 feet tall wearing a white shirt and black suit with a blue color tie having white dots on it. He said that he was not going to teach us and would keep it as an introduction class. Everybody then introduced themselves to the professor and I learnt that I had classmates from almost all the states of the country, with different religions and different graduate degrees. Well it was my turn now and I was quite nervous I stood up and introduced myself "Hello! I am Chandra Kant, I have completed my B.Com from SOL and I am from Delhi," I have been here for 3 years now, after all.

The next class was on Executive Communication, the professor was Gita Negi. When she entered the class everybody thought that she must be a newly recruited teacher as she looked too young and beautiful. What I thought was that she would not be able to handle the class. But when she started speaking everybody was quiet and paying attention to her. A lady who was5 feet in height in cream colored formals with her hair tied back, and clearly had a passion towards her work which made her more confident. After an introduction with all the students she started an activity where we have to do mimicry of any celebrity. I was very much nervous because it takes guts to do mimicry in front of 150 students and having 300 eye balls looking at you. I was busy thinking about which actor I could copy and I was not paying much attention to the class but when a guy who looked like Amir Khan came to the podium, I paid attention. Ma'am asked him to mimic any actor or celebrity he came out with the Amir Khan in him and did a fantastic mimicry of Amir Khan. This person was Nitesh Anand who was an SOL student like me and had never been to college before, looking at his guts and talent I became confident that if he could do it, I can also do it. When it was my turn I acted like Sunny Deol. I delivered the three famous dialogues of Sunny Deol – "*Tarik pe tarikh…, Mai sirf ek police officer nahi hu mai Indian hoon…, and dhai kilo ka hath…*" I don't know how the mimicry was but at the end of it everybody burst out laughing, and that's my job to make everyone smile. I missed those days when I used to be the best comedian of my school and whenever there was any function, our school teachers always included my name and asked me to prepare something to make everyone laugh.

31st August, 2011

Since we were now classmates, we three on the bus Sahiba, Simran and I introduced ourselves to each other. On this day our professor asked us to make groups of four people each, as in MBA we have to give presentation in groups, so we had to make groups. Iman and Simran and I decided to be in one group and now we needed one more partner, so Simran came up with a suggestion, it was her new friend Vatsala. I saw the girl sitting on the 3rd bench wearing a red shirt and a blue capri. Though the gal looked very low in energy, she was a studious type and I was somehow not convinced to take her in the group because of her slow voice, but we dint knew anyone else and everyone had already made their groups so I had to take her in my group. I introduced myself to Vatsala and then I came to know that she was a Psychologist and she was from Delhi itself. The phone numbers and email ids' of the group members were exchanged with each other and we were now set to prepare for the presentations.

September 2011

After one week of joining the college we were given the date of the first presentation of our group. I have never given any presentation before that, but I learned how to deliver a presentation by looking at the presentations given by my other classmates. Now as it was time for us to prepare, we all decided what needed to be done and by whom. We made a presentation and we delivered it very well on the allotted date. We were all given feedback that we had made a good presentation.

After the presentation, while having a conversation with Vatsala I asked her that being a Psychologist she must have developed some point of view about me and she said that she had. Being curious to know what a Psychologist thinks about me, I asked her to tell me what she thought. She said "Before our introduction with each other I thought that you are a 'High Achiever, introvert and an egotistical person', but when we started getting to know each other, I realized that you are a 'Goal Oriented' person who is confident enough to achieve it, and you do not trust anyone easily.; You always want things to be done in the way you want them to be done, you need instant results and get frustrated when you don't get results according to your expectations and demoralize yourself, but simultaneously you are a good leader and accept the challenges and have the capacity to win. You are also caring and have a very empathizing nature."

Listening to her I got to know a lot about myself and I was happy that I now had a good friend also, who understands me completely – in and out.

14th October, 2011

It was a regular conversation between me and Megha. She was a bit busy that day so she was disconnecting the call again and again and I was getting bored so I asked her the reason for her being so busy. She said that tomorrow is 'Karwa Chauth', the traditional Hindu festival when a wife does fast for her husband's well-being and long life. She said her mom was preparing something special for her father and she was helping her mom in that. I asked her whether she was keeping the fast for me like all other girls keep it for their boyfriends. To which she said she could but what if her mom comes to know that she had kept a fast… then she would have questions to answer, so she won't be able to. Then she asked whether I can keep the fast for her unlike other boyfriends. She knew that I can't remain hungry for even a short period of time in the day and that it would be difficult for me to remain hungry for the whole day. Though few people eat at one time during the whole day at the time of the fast, I told her that I can remain hungry for her for the whole day and that too without drinking a single drop of water. She laughed and asked me to prove it and I agreed.

15th October, 2011 (Fast)

Just before 12:00am I had some water and was prepared to keep the fast and was determined to complete it. In the morning I left for the college without having breakfast. When Mami asked me the reason behind it I told her that I am not in the mood to have breakfast so I would not have it. I went to the college and attended the classes regularly. That day, coincidentally, I had my presentation and in the presentation we have to speak a lot, while delivering the presentation I felt very thirsty but I had to survive without the water. The presentation went very well as usual and I got a positive feedback from the professor.

It was 1:30pm when the classes were over, while travelling on the metro I called up Megha and she asked me whether I had breakfast or not, when I said I didn't she said you can have food and water if you want to. She said she was happy that I can remain hungry and thirsty for her but she didn't want me to remain hungry and become ill. I said it's just a matter of few more hours and that I wanted to complete it so I will not back down.

I reached home at 3pm. and was immediately asked by Mami to have lunch. I said I had it some food in the college and she now understood the reason for not eating the food. She smiled and asked are you keeping fast for her and I told her the truth. Mami is quite frank and understands my feelings very well just like a typical Indian mom. I was feeling hungry and I usually get headache when I am hungry and my head started bursting because of the pain. Like a normal human being I thought I should eat something and Megha would never know that I have had food but my heart didn't allow me to cheat her.

At 6pm she called me and asked me if I had eaten and I said to her that I had not had anything yet. She said come to meet me outside my house. When I asked her the reason she said she wanted to meet me. I went outside her house and called her, she said she was coming out in 2 minutes. Though it was dark outside due to winter, it takes guts to come out of the house and meet your boyfriend outside your house when your family is very strict about it. She came out, smiled at me, gave me a Dairy Milk Chocolate and went inside her house again. I started my bike was going towards my apartment, she called me up and said "Before having anything to eat, please have the chocolate I gave you first and then drink some water; and I am happy that you proved what you said, **I Love You Jaan,**".

I was hungry, I was thirsty, my head was paining, and I was feeling weak, but her love made the tears of happiness come out of my eyes. My throat choked up and I couldn't speak much except for a few words **"I Love you too"**...

I reached home, had that chocolate first and then had my dinner. The chocolates tasted far better than the normal chocolates as it was given to me by Megha. She was happy that I did something which was special for her, and I was happy that she cared enough for me and gave me a chocolate of love. This only made our love stronger than ever and we were so happy to have each other.

22nd October, 2011

Megha and her cousins used to go to Ram Lila in the pre-Diwali time, and coincidentally me, Ravi and Mama, Mami also planned to visit the same Ram Lila where Megha was with her cousins. When we reached I called her up to ask where she was and she came out to see me. Mami saw Megha and said she was not beautiful but it's okay if you love her truly, beauty doesn't matter. That was the first time when I attended the Ram Lila of Delhi and I was very surprised to see that people in Delhi celebrate Ram Lila as a big event and they spend not only their money but also their time to make it a perfect celebration. Though Megha was around me for few hours but I couldn't meet her as her big brother was with her and he didn't know about us. I stayed at Ram Lila for a while but as soon as Megha left I also went home with Mama and Mami. I called her and praised her for her beauty; I told her she was looking awesome in her purple top and black jeans. She smiled and asked what Mami had said. I told my Love that Mami said that she had liked you and she was happy for us. After all Mama and Mami were going to help me ask her father to allow me to marry you. She was happy that Mami liked her and I reaffirmed to her that I was really serious about our relationship.

The Good and the Bad Year

January 2012

According to the Chinese calendar and the MAYAN calendar, the world was going to end on 12/12/2012, the news said. People had different views and thoughts about it. On being asked by Megha "What if we die, we will not be able to marry each other?"

I said "Love doesn't only means living together, it also means to die for each other, I will come to you on 12/12/2012 and we will die together so that we will always be together,"

She couldn't speak a word after this because she knew I meant what I say and I do exactly what I say.

We celebrated my birthday on the 23rd just like every year and I got a lot of gifts from her this time. These gifts played an important role in our relationships as they defined how much love we had in our hearts for our partner. She gave me a heart shaped box, which had a small book with a lot of Love quotes, she said to me "Whatever this book says is what my heart thinks about you, so do read it when you are sad, you will feel good," then there was a set of two candles, I asked her the use of those candles " she said she has a dream to go for a candle light dinner with me and she wanted me to light those candles when "We go for such dinner,"

Then there was a dancing couple globe, she said to me earnestly "This is a crystal ball which has a couple dancing in it. I hope we always remain happy and keep dancing in each other's love,"

She also gave me a coffee cup and said "I know you love coffee, but not more than me, always have your coffee in this cup you will miss me..."

And finally she had a pillow which has two hearts pierced by an arrow, she said to me "These are our hearts, which will always be together and whenever you feel alone just hug this pillow and think that it's me."

My happiness knew no bounds and no end; she loved me so much, and I could never imagine that she would think so much for me. I had the best girl in my life and I promised her that I'll never ever leave her, no matter what happened that I would always be on her side.

16th February, 2012

Though we celebrated the proposal anniversary every year, this year it was not to be enjoyed as she had some family problem. She asked me not to bring any gift for her and she told me that she would come to meet me but for a few hours only. I, being a caring boy friend, told her not to worry about anything and that I was with her in each and every decision of her life. I felt bad that we would not be able to enjoy ourselves but she being an understanding girlfriend came and met me at the Dominos' Pizza outlet at Metro Walk. We both ordered our favorite cheese burst farm house pizza and started discussing about her family problems. I tried to somehow make her understand that she didn't have anything in her hands and that maybe this year was not lucky for us, that's why everything had become bad in the very beginning. But she knew that I am always with her and she somehow convinced herself that everything would be okay on its own, thinking much about it would not solve the problem.

March 2012

One day Megha's mom suddenly asked her if she was having an affair with someone; Megha said that she wasn't have any affair with anyone. Her mother was having a strong doubt and being a religious woman she took her to the Mandir in her house and asked her to put her hand on Lord Krishna and swear that she didn't have a boyfriend. Megha was very much afraid and she swore on god that she didn't have a boyfriend. Maybe her mother was happy hearing this but Megha called me and started crying. I was worried and asked her what had happened, why was she crying? She said that she was very sad. She narrated the whole incident to me and started crying again. I was confused about what to say, I asked her if she was unhappy with the relationship, she said she is happy being with me but she doesn't like speaking lies and, cheating her parents for me. I knew what she was feeling and I understood how difficult it was for a girl to cheat her family for her boyfriend. She had to tell a lie when she came to meet her boyfriend, she had to lie when she talked to her boyfriend in the nights. She had to feel the guilt when she sleeps with her guy before marriage. She had to forget about her dreams to fulfill the dreams of her boyfriend and she had to face the relatives when they pointed their fingers at her and a whole lot of things where she had to adjust. But I couldn't do anything about it, I had two options either I leave her which I couldn't because I loved her more than anything else in this world and I knew that I cannot survive for a day without her. Another was to console her and make her understand that if we had to lie to keep our relationship alive we should not feel bad about it.

I said "I understand how much you love me. I know you have to do a lot of wrong things to keep our relationship right. I know you have to lie to keep our relationship true, you have to hide a lot of things to show me that you love me, you have to forget your dreams to make my dreams come true, you hide your tears to make me smile. You have to lose a lot of thing to get me, and I respect it, but sweet heart this is the way a relationship works and we have to lie a few times to keep our relationship alive..." This probably gave her the strength and she said "I lied not because I was afraid that my mom would shout at me hearing that I have a boyfriend, but because I never wanted to lose you.". This proved the depth of her love for me and I respected her for this.

28th May, 2012

This time we planned to celebrate her birthday in Pacific Mall, Tagore Garden. This mall has nothing new but she had a habit of visiting the places where she had never been before so she wanted to go there. Unlike all her other birthdays, this time I had a different surprise for her. I asked her to buy a top for herself as a birthday gift to keep her busy for a while and after insisting a lot she started searching for a top for herself in the different boutiques available out there. I was waiting for her to reach the top floor and she kept on visiting the shops of the ground floor. I suggested to her that she start from the shops of the top floor and she moved around the top floor slowly and entered a shop where she found something of her choice. There were different beautiful tops of different brands and after choosing a purple top she asked "How is it?" "You look beautiful in purple try it, I'll wait for you outside," I said.

She tried it and it was a perfect top for her, as always she looked gorgeous in purple. After that we came outside the shop and as we were walking towards the escalators we were just talking to each other about where to have the lunch. Suddenly we reached the middle of the top floor where I stopped her and said "Close your eyes and don't open until I say so!"

She closed her eyes and said "I am feeling very awkward closing my eyes in a public place, what are you trying to do?" I didn't speak for a while so worried that she opened her eyes and she saw me, I was bent down on my knees in front of her and gave her a red rose in front of the whole public inside the mall. I did not have any lines to speak but I could utter few words "Will you be my life forever?"

She smiled, accepted the rose and said "Yes, I will.". This way I made her smile and gave her another reason to love me.

June 2012

While doing our MBA we have to do an internship in any company of our choice for 8 weeks. The college also provide campus placements for the internship purpose but for that we have to give the interviews and get selected for the internship. I went for the interview in a very renowned company Aditya Birla Money, where I was asked a question which I could not answer.

The interviewer said "You have come to give an interview in a broking firm and you don't know the meaning of Beta, you have already completed half of your MBA and you have zero knowledge about the share market. Even if I select you, you will not be able to perform, sorry you are not selected,"

I said "Sir, I know I have completed half of my MBA but we haven't selected our field of study, the choice of which will be given to us after the internship. As the subjects related to the stock market will be taught to us in the next year, I might not have the knowledge, but I challenge that now I'll do the internship in a share broking firm and let you know that I have enough knowledge after I complete my internship,"

The interviewer laughed at me and said "I'll wait till you are back!". I took it as a challenge and I called up the Sale Manager of Sharekhan Limited, where I had my D Mat account. I told him that I have to do internship and he called me for an interview, in which I got selected and I started doing my internship there.

11th June, 2012

It was the first day of my Internship at Sharekhan Limited. I was strictly on time and wearing formals. I entered the office and the Sales Manager showed me the way to the training room. As I entered the training room the students already sitting thought that I was the trainer but I when I sit beside them they understood that

I am also a trainee. The trainer Mr. Jaipal Singh, entered the room and introduced all of us to each other. I was the only trainee from IIPM rest all were from different colleges, and the trainer started asking us few questions about the stock market before starting the training to know whether the basic concepts were clear to us or not. After asking questions to the other trainees when they could not answer the trainer used to ask me the questions which I replied very well. He praised IIPM and of course me for the knowledge I had. The internship started very well.

After few days, while having a regular conversation, Megha informed me that she has to go to Singapore for some religious functions with her cousins and family relatives and will have to be there for 10 days at least. She knew that she is going too far from me, so it will be difficult for me to live without her. I asked her if she could stay back but she wanted to go. I didn't forced her much to not to go and I said ill miss her a lot.

07th July, 2012

She was about to leave for Singapore and I knew I won't be able to see her for next 10 days; actually when you are with your partner the time runs so fast that 4 hours seems equal to 1 hour, but when you are away from her time goes so slow that one hour becomes 4hours and a week becomes a month.

I wanted to see her before she leaves Delhi so I asked her to meet me at Kohat Enclave Metro station. I was on the way to Kohat and I was driving my bike very fast, in a hurry to reach her so that we could spend some more time with each other. Of course a single minute meant a lot to me at that time as she had come for few minutes only. While driving at that time I hated all the red lights and those people who were driving too slow as they were wasting my time which I could spend with my sweetheart. I was about to reach Kohat Enclave and suddenly I found myself hit by two cars from both the sides, I felt like nothing has happened and started the bike again, I tried to change the gear but I couldn't, damn! I was hurt; my left leg was paining so much that I couldn't change the gear but I knew I had to meet her and for that I had to do all that I could. I somehow gathered the energy to change the gear and reached the destination, but before she could see me I wanted to check my jeans whether everything was alright or not. Because I did not wanted her to get worried about me and I knew if she gets worried then she would not be able to enjoy her vacation, I parked my bike on the service lane and I stood up nearby, but I wasn't able to stand properly, maybe I have got a dislocation of the bones or some hairline fracture or maybe it's just a strain or sprain but whatever it is I have to hide it from her and walk properly in front of her.

I somehow managed to walk towards her car and I did not have any expression of pain on my face, she asked me is everything alright and I smiled and said yes everything is alright. I held her hand and I kept looking at her. A few seconds after looking at her, I felt like all my pain went away, I felt liked nothing had happened. She was started feeling shy as I was continuously looking at her. She smiled and said please don't look at me like this, and I wanted her to see more and more as her smile worked as a painkiller for me.

I smiled and said I want to spend my whole life looking at you sweetheart, would you allow me to look into your eyes and feel your love for me. She smiled mischievously and said "No, you are not allowed to look at me, so turn your face and stop looking at me," I kept my right hand on the back of her neck and my left hand on her right hand, I started moving close to her and I kissed her forehead, moving my lips from her forehead to her lips I said "I want to be with you forever and I know you too want to be with me forever," I kissed her and that kiss was just like a drink of heaven after which I have to go back to the earth and spend a month without her, yes 10 days were just like a month for me.

She hugged me and said "I'll miss you and I'll call you if I get cellular network in the sea..." Soon I realized that once I had been to cruise earlier and the cell phone would not be working when the ship is offshore and we could get the network only while the ship is nearby some port. So it was another bad news for me that we would not be able to talk to each other and even if she gets the network somewhere the cousins and family relatives will be around her so maybe she would not be able to call me, but I asked her go give me a call if she could. She knew how difficult it was for me to survive without talking to her for so many long days. She said don't worry sweetheart I'll take care of myself and you too take care of yourself. The coming 10 days will teach us the importance of each other and while I am enjoying the trip you will enjoy the internship and be happy. Is that okay? She asked me. I said yes, I will take care of myself and will wait for your call. She said I Love You and after I replied her back, she left.

09th July, 2012 (Day 3 without her)

Wondering how is she I was on the way to my office, I dint knew when I reached the office and I was inside the training room. I was physically present in the training room but mentally I was lost somewhere else, maybe I was worried about her, or maybe I was feeling alone without her, suddenly my trainer turned his face towards me and said Isn't it CK?? I said umm, yes. He said you are lost somewhere else today isn't it CK?? And you replied, yes. Everyone burst out in laughter.

The best thing which I liked in me was, I was just like an open book, and everyone everywhere who knew me knew about my relationship, I never hide anything because I never could. As every time I had to talk to her on phone and there was no use of telling people that it was someone else not a girlfriend, it's better to tell a single truth in place of thousands of lies. The other trainees in the training room knew that I was badly missing my girlfriend and that is why I couldn't concentrate and whenever I used to look at them in between the training sessions they used to smile at me.

Oh God! is this the Love fever, I was completely out of the control of my mind. I tried calling on her cell phone after the class was over but it was not reachable.

12th July, 2012 (Day 6 without her)

Despite knowing the fact that there is only One percent chance that she would be able to call me up, I always kept my phone with me and that too on ringing mode. Even inside the training room sometimes my phone use to rang and the trainer would get angry on me, but he knew that I was not behaving properly since last few days so he kept mum on this. When I was at my home my phone rang and when her dad's number flashed on my phone's screen I rubbed my eyes again to make myself believe that it is she. I received the call and I could hear the voice which I was missing from last 6 days which were equal to 24 days for me. I asked her about her well-being, and she said she is fine and enjoying a lot. Though I was angry on her and I wanted to shout on her for not calling me, but I already knew the reason behind it so I did not show my anger.

Did you miss me? She asked.

Of course I did my Jaan. Did you?

No. I didn't as I was not free to miss you, she replied mischievously.

Though this type of reply when I expect something else irritates me, but when she replies in such a way and then smiles and being asked by me the same question again she gives the expected reply, I become happy.

I asked her again did u miss me Jaan?

Yes, of course I do sweetheart. All the cousins are around and I have to call my dad also so I need to disconnect the call.

Okay! Do take care of yourself, do call me if you get the network again, and I'll miss you a lot, Love You.

Okay! Ill, you too take care, I'll miss you too, Love you Too. I was dying to listen to these three magical words Love You Too in her melodious voice and I felt very relaxed after this conversation with her. It worked just like an oxygen mask in a planet where there is no oxygen and I was dying without it.

16th July, 2012 (Day 10)

As usual it was an office day, I just completed the work and about to leave the office when she called me up. Hello! I am back. She said.

Though I was eagerly waiting for her call and was dying to listen to her voice, I behaved in a very awkward manner. I said I don't want to talk to you. When she asked the reason, I said, because you called me only once in those 10 days which were equal to 40 days for me. I knew the reason behind her not being able to call me up but I was very much alone these days and I somehow got angry on her without any reason and that's the worst part of my behavior. I am short tempered and then I don't realize what all I did in last few minutes when I was angry on someone.

I shouted on her but after a small argument on the very same topic she somehow convinced me to meet her the next day. This was the best part of our relationship, whenever I became angry on her she talked to me with so much of love that I melted like ice. I was happy because it was rare from her side that she asks me to meet her, otherwise I was the one who always asked her to come to meet me.

17th July, 2012

The next day I was waiting for her at Kohat Enclave, as soon as she was with me, my eyes were seeking my hearts permission to see her from top to bottom so that they could get a rest from the pain of not being able to see her from last 10 days. I was spellbound sitting next to her in her car, I was busy in looking at her and a few drops of happiness came out of my eyes. She wiped those tears and asked, "Why do you love me so much? *Pagal hai kya?*"

I replied, "*Haan hoon pagal, tere pyar mein…*"

She smiled and hugged me, and I kissed her on her lips without even thinking that we were in a public place and someone might see us doing this. When I am with her I forget everything except one thing, that I am with her and I love her a lot. She then started telling me about her tour, the people she met, the things which she did in those days, the weather and all about how she enjoyed those days, but I was busy in looking at her sweet innocent face, her smile and her black silky hair coming on her face and she was helping them behind her ears with her fingers.

Then she told me about how they all danced on the cruise, and then I shared my memories with her when I was on a cruise with my school teachers and class mates on a organized school trip, and how we all enjoyed that night. Then I told her I wish to learn how to dance and that too with her. She then suggested me to join some dance classes, and I asked her if she could join the same with me. She agreed and I started searching for the dance classes the very next day. She took her mother's permission for the dance classes and soon we both joined the Salsa dance classes as a couple we had our pair.

Day 01 – Salsa Classes

This was the best way to fulfill the desire to spend time with her, during these dance classes she will be with me for one hour everyday which may complete the emptiness of those long 10 days without her. As usual she was late and I was waiting for her, to wait for her was the best moment of my life because those long few minutes made me realize how important she was for me and how much I love her. She parked her car and we both went inside the classes together. The teacher was a female; she was looking simple in her red T-shirt and black stretchable legging, her hair were oily and tied back on her head, her triangular face cut was missing the charm because of work stress, but somehow she was able to manage everything with her smile. She came to us and she asked if we both are couples, to which we happily agreed, she smiled and said very few are lucky to learn salsa with their real partner.

Then she started teaching us with the basics and asked me to hold her right hand with the left hand and put my right hand on her waist. This was may be the first time when we were so close in front of someone but we had to. She taught us the four basics and asked us to practice the same at home, I wish I could take you home for the practice I said to Megha, and she said shut up with a smile. This was a trial class and we both were comfortable with everything so we agreed to continue it further.

Day 07 – Salsa Classes

We were love birds and we always kept searching for the "Vella" (free) time to meet each other and love each other, that day we planned to meet outside the dance classes a few minutes before the classes and we kept sitting inside the car for those few minutes. When we entered the class and the teacher asked us "you both were sitting inside the car, why dint you came inside the class if you were before time?" Me and Megha looked and each other and smiled, and the teacher understood the reason and she also smiled. This was the day when we were closer than any other day of the dance classes, as today the teacher knew that we were in true love and she need not shy teaching us the closest possible steps of salsa, were I need to pick her up, where I need to hug her and where I need to take her in my arms and a lot more like that.

Day 15 – Salsa Classes

The last day of Salsa classes, we both were having mixed emotions. We were happy because today we had learned one art of dancing and we were sad because we would no more be able to meet daily like in the past 15 days. Me and Megha both wanted to enjoy this last day of salsa classes to the fullest, the teacher taught us the ball room steps where I have to take her in my arms, where I had to pick her up and the way we danced that day was awesome, I never knew we both would become such a good dancers. Then she requested the teacher to play "Pehla nasha, Pehla Khumar", her favorite song, and she wanted me to dance with her on that song. The beautiful song, the beautiful lightings, the beautiful moment and of course the beautiful partner to dance with. The song got played again and again because of few mistakes done by us, as we were not doing the steps along with the track, but when we both realized that we were with each other, hand in hand and we wanted to do the same dance in our marriage with each other in the future, we wanted to give our best. This time when the song got played, we danced, we enjoyed the lyrics, the track, the belongingness of each other and the love was in the air, we danced to the fullest and we dint even recognized when did the song finished, and everyone out there started clapping for us. Teacher was happy to see us both dancing so well, with so much of true emotions and more than that the love for each other.

12th October, 2012 (Friday)

Every Friday we had Business Policy Classes for 3 hours in the college so we had to wear formals. As usual I boarded the college bus from NSP, I was listening to my favorite songs and due to the traffic jam which in not so usual in the early mornings, that day we were late. I was feeling very uncomfortable in the bus, I was sweating which I thought may be because of the climate, it was very uneasy in the formals and I was getting low in energy which may be because of not having breakfast in the morning I thought. Slowly and a bit late we reached the college, by "we" I mean Simran, my class mate and me, as she also used to come in the same bus.

We entered the class after checking the schedule; the class room was full and chilled. I made myself comfortable near Vatsala, my best friend and of course a few common friends were also sitting nearby. The class started as usual with a quite serious note. Suddenly I started feeling too cold and weak, I was very much low on energy. I wanted to pee but the professor was so strict that I knew he would not allow me to go out except in the breaks. When the teacher turned towards the white board I shifted to the back bench thinking that, at the back side there must be less cold. But it could not help me out, it was still very cold and I was freezing, I asked one of my class mate if he is also feeling the same, he nodded his head in yes so I thought the ac temperature is very low, somehow I managed till the break.

As soon as the break was announced I rushed to the canteen and got a Limca. Looking at me my friends suggested that I might be having low BP because of which I am low in energy and Limca would work as a stimulator. I had Limca, but then I had to rush towards the washroom as I felt like vomiting; I was confused on what to do, nothing like that ever happened to me.

After the class of BP I went to the reception to ask for a medicine for fever, as I was feeling cold even outside the class where it was too hot.

For a moment I wanted to go home but then I realized that it's a matter of next 2 hrs, I should attend the class and attendance were also too important so somehow I managed to attend the next class also. As soon as the class was over, I took the college but to the metro station and boarded the metro. It was a journey of 1 hr. from Qutub Minar Metro Station to Rohini East Metro, which was hell long for me that day as I was not able to even stand properly and I hadn't got any seat to sit. As soon as the train entered Pratap Nagar Metro Station I came out of metro and sat on a chair on the platform, I was so weakened that was couldn't stand for few more seconds. I took my cell phone out and called Megha.

Hello!

Hello!

Hello! Are u there?

Hellooo, yaar I am not able to speak up.

What happened, where are you?

I am at Pratap Nagar Station, I am sitting on a chair, I cannot stand I am feeling very much low and I think I am not even able to speak.

Why? What happened to you?

I don't Know, I think it's a viral as I am feeling very cold in Metro and I…

And you? Speak up baby, achha do one thing, just get out of Metro Station and hire an auto to reach home.

Umm… I can't, I am sure I will not get auto from here and even they will not take me home as I am not well, so nobody would take a risk. Even if I don't get an auto I can't stand for a long time as I am not able to.

Just try to get an auto if you can, otherwise reach home through metro asap and when you reach home go to the dr. immediately.

Hmm… I am getting inside the train again and I would call you when I reach home.

Okay take care, do call me when you reach home, Love you.

Love you too.

I was again standing inside the metro; a policeman was standing in front of me. I thought I should ask him for help but then I realized I was just a miles away from my home and Mami is alone at home, so if the policeman takes me to the hospital, it will be very difficult for Mami to manage everything. I called up Mami and asked her to be ready to take me to the doctor as I wanted to see a dr. as soon as I reach my apartment. She got a bit worried and finished up everything hurriedly, when I reached to my bike which was parked at Netaji Subhash Palace Metro Station I was a bit feeling better; I somehow gathered the energy to drive the bike till I reached home. We went to the dr. and then he said "I guess you have dengue, I am giving you some medicines and I have written some tests on the prescription, which you need to get done today and show me the reports by tomorrow". I got those tests done; I went home and called up Megha as I knew she must be worried and waiting for my call. I told her everything will be alright and she also acted very much unworried in order to relax my mood and said "Yes sweetheart when I am with you, nothing wrong will happen to you, so don't worry and take some rest".

I had dinner but I couldn't sleep the whole night as I was feeling very weak and helpless. I couldn't even call Megha as she would get angry on me for not taking rest and I also dint have sufficient energy to utter a word. As advised by the dr. I was having a lot of water because of which I had to go to washroom again and again which probably disturbed Mami also. But I was very worried to see myself like this, I never felt like this ever in my life.

13th October, 2012

The reports were ready; the platelet count was 145000 which was less than the minimum platelets required in a human body. The dr. was surprised to see that even I such situation I was able to ride my bike, take the reports from the diagnostic centre and go to the dr. to show the reports. He said when the platelets are less than the required a person doesn't have energy to even carry himself properly how come you drive your bike and manage everything. I smiled and said, "I don't know". It was awkward for me, I knew there was something very wrong but then he suggested me to get blood tests twice a day and show him the reports every day. Till then I had to take medicines and a lot of liquids too.

I was worried, tensed, weakened, lost, but I wanted to meet Megha. I asked her if somehow she could meet me. But neither she could do and nor did my Mami allowed me to go outside till I am okay. Mami was just like my mother for me, she took care for me, she brought a lot of cold drinks, coconut water, glucose, and every possible thing of the world which could help me in getting alright. I even started hating the chapatti's, which is normal when you have dengue. She made every possible food which I may like to eat but I had to be alive on liquids and only liquids and have to go to rest room every now and then.

The nurses on the diagnostic centre started feeling sorry for me as every day they have to take blood from my veins twice and I was like a one man army, I had to get the tests done, take the reports and show to the dr. daily. Though Mami always wanted to go along with me but I never took her along with me as she had a child to look after, my cousin Sujal.

15th October, 2012

The platelet count was getting lower, it reached 132000, the situation was worst. Dr. said it is dengue but he will not admit me to the hospital until the platelet counts goes more down as according to him sometimes patients recover without the hospitalization. I started feeling itching on my legs and palm in the mid night. Everyone at home was slept, I took a towel, poured some water on it and rubbed that wet towel on my legs and palm, thinking that there might be some itching because of not taking bath from last 3 days. But I got no relief from it, I took out some Nycil powder and applied it, but alas, nothing is working. I kept scratching the palm and legs the whole night like a monkey but I had no other option. I called Megha but she dint picked up the phone, her cell phone was on silent mode she replied the next day.

16th October, 2012

At the platelet count of 127000, it started all over again. Oh my god, what the hell is happening to me, I never did anything wrong to anyone. Why me I started crying and shouting when Mami came and rubbed my legs and palm till I felt a bit better. I even started hating the smell of the food getting cooked in the kitchen, but I had to bear it as I have no other option. Mami wanted me to eat something as I haven't had food since last 2 days but the neighbor made her understand that this is a symptom and its better if I take liquids only.

17th October, 2012

Now the platelet count was 120000, where I was weak, feeling cold, itching in the palm and legs. I was taken to the hospital where I again had to go through the blood tests. The dr. diagnosed me, Smiled and uttered few words "He is having dengue, we have to admit him". A few drops of tears came out of my eyes, I was feeling like I would not get out of this hospital alive now, those days were like the last few days of my life. They took me to the room; put a syringe in my left hand which was taking the glucose inside my body, twice or thrice and sometimes multiple times the nurses used to give me injections of some liquid medicines. I had never been to any hospital before and at least never as a patient except once when I had a severe stomach ache when I was in hostel a few years back. I informed Megha that I am admitted in the hospital and I am not allowed to keep the cell phone inside the room, she can call Mami to get updates on my well-being. She was tensed, silent and she asked me to take care of myself. May be she was crying thinking that I am very serious but she dint show it to me, she said "everything will be alright and get well soon to meet me, I will be waiting for you sweetheart, I Love You".

Those three words looked like the last words from her as I thought I'll never be able to see or talk to her anymore, I don't know why I lost the battle without fighting, maybe just because it was the first time when I was attacked by such a serious disease and I was afraid of dying.

Bade Mamaji (Shiv Mami) was informed about my illness; he is the eldest among all my relatives and has more knowledge of everything than the others in the family. He came along with Mami and they enquired about the condition, the medicines prescribed, the treatment given and everything needed. I was more relaxed to see him as he takes care that nothing goes wrong with the treatment and of course when the eldest in the family is with you, your tension transfers to him. The platelet count in the evening reached 84000 and the dr. relaxed everyone by saying that currently the situation is not much serious and there is nothing to worry about.

By the night everyone went back to their home except Mahesh Mamaji who insisted to stay along with me in the hospital. The nurses were coming to change the glucose bottles in the night and many times I had to call them to remove the drip as I had to pee again and again due to the excess of cold and the glucose also. A sleepless night, without the phone and without talking to her, but I was more concerned about her, I dint wanted her to panic thinking about my illness, but I had nothing to do and I had to spend that whole night thinking what all I will do if I would be okay once again or what if I die.

18th October, 2012

It was the day when my mom dad was arriving to see me. Shiv Mamaji came early that day to check the reports and the platelet count again dropped to 84000, to which the dr. said that I have to be ready for the worst where I could get red rashes on my body, a lot of itching and more than that. Mom and Dad arrived, I was never so weak that I would not be able to stand up and touch their feet. They enquired about the reports and my mom's face turned pale after hearing that the situation is getting worst. Dad was silent, he never said anything to me and I dint expected him to say anything too, as if he would have dropped a single tear out of his eyes, it would have broken me from inside. The nurses again took the blood samples in front of my mom's eyes and she could not see me in pain, but she had no choice too. Then arrived Dimpal Mami, for whom I was waiting, I was waiting to hear from her that Megha called her up and asked her for my well-being. When dad went back home, and only me, mom and Mami was inside the room, Mami told me that Megha is worried and she wanted to come and see me. I smiled and asked my Mami to tell her not to come today as Shiv Mamaji is here and he would get angry to know about my relationship and if possible she can come tomorrow morning.

After few minutes when I was alone with my mom in the room I burst out crying. She too was emotional and worried but she said don't worry I am here everything will be alright. In the evening the dr. reported that the platelets are further decreasing and the count has reached 64000 and then he smiled and said something which gave me strength to fight. He said "I you lose hope, no one can save you from dying; but if you want to survive, you will get the energy to fight and win".

Then I started collecting the reasons why I have to live, I have to live to fulfill my mother's dream of seeing me become something great, I have to live for myself to fulfill my duty towards my parents, I have to live to fulfill the dreams of Megha who is eagerly waiting to see me, I have to live to fulfill the promises made to her and I have to live because I was born to do something for which I have been given the birth of a Human Being. Those reasons gave me energy to fight, to battle and win.

This time my mom decided to stay along with me and Mahesh Mamaji also decided to stay as we needed someone to be there with us in case of emergency. Again the scary restless night, the nurses doubling the doses of medicines, and suddenly the itching started in the palms and the legs. I told my mom about the itching, she started rubbing my legs and the palms, for about half an hour she did so and then the itching stopped and I was able to sleep for half an hour after which I had to go to washroom again and again when for which my mom had to call the nurse now and then to remove the drips. Again the itching started and again my mom tried to relax it by rubbing my hands and legs, I worked out again but this time it didn't go completely, it decreased to a bearable level. I was afraid of the rashes and the decreasing platelets count but I was positive that tomorrow the platelet count is going to increase and I am going to be fine by the next day, maybe it was my sixth sense or the will to survive, but somehow that long night ended.

19th October, 2012

The morning made me feel better as today I expected Megha to come. Mom went home to have breakfast leaving behind Dimpal Mami who brought some juice and my cell phone for me. She said Megha wants to talk to you and of course I was waiting for her to tell me when Megha is about to come and suddenly the unexpected happened, Shiv Mamaji and Mamiji came early that day and I knew now Megha won't be able to come to see me. Shiv Mamaji asked me about my well-being and said he is getting a positive feeling that I am going to be alright very soon. I sent a message to Megha that she should not come to meet me as Bade Mamaji has come to the hospital and he would get angry if he comes to know about us. She was alright with it as she got the news that I am recovering and will be okay very soon. I was unhappy because I wanted Megha to come to see me but she couldn't and I was happy because I was feeling better today than those past few days.

The reports came and the dr. said "The platelet counts have increased to 72000 and it's a sign of recovery". I could see a smile on my Dad's face after hearing this and everyone was taking care of me like never before. I remember what Megha used to say sometimes "I was to get unwell for few days, not because I want to take some rest, just because I want everyone to take care of me a lot and I would feel like a queen". I know this sounds childish but it's the truth, it was working with me. I smiled and I laughed a lot, I started cracking jokes with everyone and I was jumping off the bed as I was recovering and I was happy to see myself better. Actually the happiness was because I wanted to get well to meet Megha, to be in her arms once again and to roam around with her and spend time with her, to kiss her, to hug her, to enjoy the best of my life with her.

The reports in the evening brought some good news once again where the platelet count increased to 122000 and the dr. promised me to discharge me of the platelets reaches the 150000 mark "A minimum count of platelets required in human body". The itching stopped, the weakness ended and I was feeling better, better and better.

In the night, Mom stayed with me and she told me how my Uncle was worried about me when he heard that I am hospitalized, how everybody back home was worried and how each and every relative of ours were taking the updates about me frequently.

20th October, 2012

Someone informed us that Shiv Mamaji is not coming today as he has got some work, the other relatives were there and now Megha could come to meet me, but hang on! The dr. has brought the reports and he said "Congratulations! Your platelet count has reached the count of 151000 and you are fit and fine to go home now". He asked Mahesh Mamaji to get the discharge papers ready and clear the dues, which they did in few hours and I was allowed to go home at 12pm.

I informed Megha that I have been discharged and I am absolutely fit and fine now. She was happy to hear this and I was waiting for her call to make a plan to meet her, but I was not allowed to go out of home today as mom and dad were waiting for me at home and Dad was about to leave for Rajasthan. I went home to see off Dad, and then my mom and Mami started taking care of me like a small baby, they started filling my tummy every now and then with different types of juices and liquids thinking that I still have some weakness in my body.

I was feeling better than before, far better than what I was before having the Dengue. I opened my almirah at my home and wanted to see the things which were kept inside it. I jumped to the gifts given by Megha at my birthday's which I used to keep inside my almirah and I was looking at them. I found something unusual; the dancing couple globe was broken, it was the closest of all of them. I was hurt, I asked Mami who did that but she said no one touched my almirah except her and that to only once when I asked her to do so. She said she did not touched the gifts and I doubted on Ankit (Mami's brother) who has come to stay with us for few days, but I could not say anything to him as I had no proof.

I called up Megha and I was afraid that she is going to get angry on hearing this, but when I told her that someone has broken that gift. She said, "It's just a gift sweetheart, so what if it's broken, at least you have the most precious gift of your life 'Me' with you". I smiled and then she asked me what all I did in the hospital and I enquired about what all she did in my absence and how much we missed each other in those days when we both were not able to talk to each other. Actually these types of distances, makes us understand and feel the importance of the special someone in our life.

November 2012 (Yet another Simran)

I don't remember the date, but it's not much important also. Simran Chawla, my classmate, she was a good friend of mine till that day. By 'That Day' I mean the day when I realized that she is giving special importance to me in each and everything. Each and everything means the special attention, whether I have had food in time. Whether I have done my assignment in time or not, showing me that she is performing better in the presentations, showing me that she is contributing very much in our group, she is doing exactly what I wanted her to and then she started getting jealous of Megha when Megha used to call and message me when I was with her.

Once, when I was travelling to my college in the same college bus in which we (Me and Simran) used to, she was sitting beside me. She started the topic of Megha, she wanted to know each and everything about us and then I discussed what all happened after Megha came into my life including the two proposals which I got in the past. Then she started telling me what all is good about me and what all she likes about me which made me feel good, of course anyone would be happy hearing good things about himself. She also told me about the relationship she had with a guy who left her in tears a few years back.

Then she asked me what do I think about her and I told her that she is a good friend of mine and I love all my friends but I love Vatsala more than anyone else. I appreciated the way Simran used to care for me but this is not what I expected from her, a good friend does care but up to some extent and not above the limits which I asked her not to do so, and then she started crying which made me speechless. I held her hand and tried to calm her down when she told me that she Loves me and she wants me to be her Boy Friend.

For a while I was feeling like I am Shahrukh Khan and all the girls named as Simran were falling in love with me. But trying to be a bit serious, I told her that she knows that I am already in relationship and that too since almost 4 years, which is a true and serious relationship from both the ends, how could she expect me to leave Megha and get into a relationship with her, she was silent and then

I said "I always took you as a good friend of mine but hereafter I would not be able to consider you as a good friend of mine, because my closeness with you is going to hurt you more and if I still remain your friend I would never be able to talk to you the way I used to". Once again tears of pain came scrolling down from her eyes, but this time I couldn't help, because helping her would maybe hurt Megha which I could never allow to happen.

We reached the college and then we separated to different seats, Vatsala came to know that there is something wrong with Simran and when she looked at me she sensed that may be I would have said something hurtful to her which may be related to her performance in the group or the presentations. But until I shared everything with her she dint knew anything, Vatsala knew the decision I took was right and she knew how much loyal I was in my relationship and of course as a friend of Simran, she consoled her and tried to make her understand that I was right and she had to understand the reality.

This was the Third and Last proposal till date and I never wanted to hurt any one of them but I couldn't help out. I told Megha about what all happened throughout the day and she was really surprised to know that I again have got a proposal. To pinch me she said, "*Yaar tu itna to achha hai bhi nahi jitney tujhe ladkiya propose kar deti hai, pata nai kya dekhai deta hai unko tujhme,*" and started laughing. This is the reason why I loved her more than anyone else in my life as she was the best gal I could ever be in relationship with. If she could have got a proposal from someone I could have got angry on her thinking that there must be something wrong with her behavior with that guy because of which he had proposed her or I would have become over protective in some case. But she, she was totally different from me, and as you know Opposites Attracts. The dissimilarity between both of us brought us together and despite of having different thought process we were together and we were in the depth of love with each other.

The next day onwards Simran started sitting to the different seat in the bus, she stopped even smiling at me while entering inside the bus, she was ignoring me but when she used to sit on the front seat in the class she used to stare at me with her wet eyes while I used to sit on the back seats just to stay away from her. The only medium of conversation between us was the group conversation during the preparation of some assignment or project. All of this continued to a very long time, meanwhile I had a fight with one of my group member Alex after which Vatsala and few other friends of mine stopped talking to me or maybe I thought that being my best friend if Vatsala doesn't behave nicely with me I should never ever go and talk to anyone of them.

I even stopped replying to Text Messages of Simran and blamed Simran for all those misunderstandings and fights between me, Vatsala and all other friends of mine. I was separated from my own group and I hated Simran for taking my best friend away from me. I was very angry on Vatsala for not being with me and I thought that she has changed and she doesn't consider me her best friend anymore. Then I joined a completely different group with Nitesh (The Amir Khan Copy of my class who acted as Amir Khan in the very first class of Executive Communication).

I used to hang out with my new friends and but then I used to feel bad about the friendship of me and Vatsala going towards an end which I never wanted to, she was an support to me in the college as I used to share everything with her and suddenly she was not there with me and I had no one to hear me and understand the way I used to think. She was the one who always took me for granted and used to say that whatever I did was right, this was not because she never wanted to go against me or she wanted to show me that she cares for me but, this was because being a Psychologist she understands that the way I think I was right was absolutely correct from my part.

She knew the process of my work and she used to appreciate the way I used to do it, she used to help me in everything and used to contribute a lot to the group tasks assigned to us but seeing her in a completely different mood and behavior I was a bit upset. Megha suggested me to clear things up with Vatsala and talk to her but I never wanted to do so, after all I had my male ego superseding the friendship.

12/12/12

As we promised each other on the beginning of the year, that if the world ends today we will die together. So we were there at our favorite place called as Khopcha, an empty road near the ZP Block park where we used to park our car and spend a lot of time with each other alone. As usual I was 15 min before the time to check whether the place is all vacant and there is no one else to see us and disturb us and she was 15 minutes late by the time, ultimately I had to wait for half an hour for her.

When she arrived I asked her to come on time or inform me if she is late so that I do not have to wait for so long. This was a formality now, as she never reached on time and I always had to wait, and that wait for her reminded me of those long 18 years of my life after which she came into my life. I usually cannot wait for anyone but I always waited for her and it was awesome moment of my life as it increased my urge to see her, to feel her breath around me and to love her more. She knew that I am short tempered and I become impatient when I had to wait for her, but she also knew that after a few lines of anger which I utter, I become calm and I say sorry for getting angry on her.

We were sitting inside the car and were lost in talking with each other and then we realized that a PCR is standing in front of us in which 2 police man and a lady constable were sitting, looking at us. I asked Megha to start the car and try to cross that PCR by side if they could let us go, otherwise they are going to take us to the police station and call our families out there. She started the engine and tried to cross that PCR to get out of that road but the PCR driver dint let her cross the PCR and stopped us.

The Policeman on the other side came out of the PCR and he called me to come out of the car, I asked Megha to keep sitting until I ask her to come out. The police man asked me what we two were doing on the empty road to which I replied humbly that Megha is just practicing the car and I was guiding her on how to park a car. He said, he is not a fool, he asked me to show him my license which I showed and then he asked for Megha's license which she dint had.

He called Megha out but I asked her to be seated inside the car no matter what happens, Megha kept sitting inside the car and the police man was surprised to see that she dint came out when the police is asking her out. He asked me whether we were couples and we were meeting here, to which I replied yes we were and we just came and parked the car when you people arrived. He then asked me for my Name and mobile number of my local guardians, I gave him mobile no. of Sunil Mamaji and then the other policeman asked Megha for to tell her name and her father's mobile number.

She started crying and she looked at me, I said don't utter a single word even if they take us to the police station and the police man were surprised to see that after that she dint utter a single word, this is the level of trust she had on me, she knew even in the worst I would handle everything and will not let her down. I asked the policeman to come to me and ask me whatever he wants to ask, he came to me and asked me her name and mobile no. of her dad. He threatened me to take us to the police station and call our family if I don't give him the information.

When I saw Megha crying, tears came out of my eyes too and then with an innocent voice and in a very low tone, I told the policeman that her name is Megha and her family doesn't know anything about our relationship, so if I give him the information and he calls up her family then our relationship would end and ill die without her. I promise him ill never come to this place again if they allow us to go without taking any action on us. I told him that he could take me to the police station and charge me with anything which he wants to, he could give me any punishment even give me a life time imprisonment but let her go home, I cannot see her crying. The police man's heart filled with emotions to see both of us crying and being so much in love with each other, he saluted me for dying to save her from everything and he said, "There are very few couples in this world whose bonding is so strong, you both are crying for each other and you are ready to do anything just to stop her from crying, this is what true love means."

They let us go and advised us to not to sit in the places where there is no one to save us from any unforeseen situation. There are many crimes reported where the girl and boy are alone and the girl gets harmed by someone else and the boy gets either beaten or charged for the wrong things happened to the girl. We both agreed to them and promised that we would not meet in such places hereafter and would meet each other in public places.

She drove car towards the Netaji Subhash Palace Metro Station and parked the car there, she said "We will not meet on empty places like that hereafter and I want to go home now if you don't feel bad". I looked at her, she was flinched and very silent and I could still see a few drops of tears coming out of her eyes. I held her hand and said "It's okay, we have not committed any crime to be in relationship with each other, and this world has two types of people. One, who understands everything and go with the trend and the other who are against the relationships. We have these hurdles just because we are living in a society where the love and relationships are still considered as wrong thing but it doesn't mean that we should stop loving each other, we have come this far and I would never want anyone of us to leave in between just because the society doesn't accept it. I know anything would have happened today but somehow we are out of it and we would take care of it that such situation doesn't come again, and you know what I'll go against the whole world to be with you and I don't care if I had to do anything to be your forever".

She looked at me, hugged me and said, "I am the luckiest girl who has you as a boy friend in my life and trust me I'll always be with you no matter what, but '*mere papa ko tu hi manaega, mai kuchh nahi bolungi*'," and she smiled. This was the best part of her nature when she put humor in the sadistic situations and make me smile when I least expect it. It was very hot outside and the car AC wasn't working properly so I asked her to go home, relax and not to think much about today's incident.

She smiled at me and I smiled at her, we both had a short lip kiss, a close hug and she left for her home.

In the Rain

16th February, 2013

It was our 4th Proposal Anniversary; we had already decided that we are going for a date and that too for a coffee at Starbucks which just opened up a week back in Connaught Place (Delhi). As usual we met each other at Kohat the Place of Love, I wore the Purple Sweater which she gifted me a month's back on my birthday, a bit loose in fitting. Loose because she went to Stanmax with her college friends Nitika and Sakshi, she thought if she would ask for the size 'Small' then her friends may laugh on her so she asked for the 'Medium' size and asked nitika to try it. Nitika tried it and it was perfect in size for her, and Megha bought it for me, the color purple which I never wore and which I dint even liked.

Now because it was gifted by her I had to wear a sweater which was loose in size and a different color which I never wore. When she saw me wearing that sweater she laughed and said if this isn't fitting you why did u wore it, I said just because you gave it with love I had to wear it and in future when we get married and you have to choose the clothes for me you just see to it that you choose the right size for me. She kept on laughing constantly and when I asked the reason behind it she narrated me the story that a guy's sweater was tried by a girl and just because it was fit on her, I would fit me as well I burst into laughter too.

While she was driving I was looking at her, I always do this and she hated this, really, when you are constantly looking at a girl she hates it as she feels a bit shy or some of them think that there is something wrong with her dress up or the makeup. She said, "Yaar please stop stalking me." and she sneaked a look at the front mirror of the car and checked whether her lip gloss and eye liner is applied properly or her hair is well tied. I again looked at her and smiled to which she said, "Now what?"

I enjoyed when she gets worried about her dress up and finally the question which I was expecting from her, "*Main kaisi lag rahi hoon?*"

You are looking amazing sweet heart, no one in this world could give you competition except one, and I smiled again. She curiously asked, "Except One? Who is that?" and I didn't say anything and kept quiet until she asked me again, "Who is she?"

Before she gets angry I had to tell her, "You yourself sweetheart." She smiled and said, "*Koi aur hoti to mai uski jaan le leti.*" After all every time it was her who did such mischief and this time I took the spot.

We reached Starbucks; we have never been to that place earlier, a different theme of the restaurant and the mesmerizing fragrance of coffee beans which reminds me of a Hollywood movie in which the couple had coffee in the same glass and their romance started with that cup of coffee. I asked Megha to order till I search a perfect seat for both of us, she ordered the coffee and our names were written on those coffee glasses. She took the glass on which her name was written and gave me the one on which my name was written. We were sitting beside each other instead of sitting on front of each other unlike any other couple. The reason being, when we are sitting in front of each other we are just able to see each other but when we are sitting beside each other we can hold each other's hand.

We looked and each other and we exchanged our glasses, now Megha was with me and I was with Megha. In short we were in each other's hand, after few sips of coffee we again exchanged our glasses, and the reason was simple, the coffee becomes tastier when we have the lip prints of our love on our straw. Of course because it was a restaurant we couldn't have the coffee in one glass otherwise it would have been the best option to feel the belongingness of each other.

The best place, the best coffee, the best date with the best partner of this world, I was happy and was feeling lucky to have her in my life.

We came back to the Kohat Metro Station and she was about to leave when I asked her to stay there for few more minutes, it was our anniversary and how could I let her go so easily without a hug and a kiss. Like all other places we had a secret place there too, to meet and spend time with each other. It was just few steps away from the metro station where we parked our car and were sitting inside the car.

It was complete silence in the car and I was constantly looking at her, to break the silence she asked "How was the coffee?"

I was like, the coffee? Seriously? I said "Close your eyes and let me tell you how was it". She closed her eyes and I kissed her, the coffee was awesome but not more than you.

It was a bit cold outside and when we sit inside a car without switching on the AC, the fog starts turning the car glasses cloudy from inside, then neither we were able to see outside nor anybody from outside was able to see us.

Megha was about to switch on the AC, I stopped her from doing that and I held her left hand in my right hand, our eyes met and it was a complete silence from both the ends. She was on the driver's seat and I was on her left, I slightly moved towards her a bit uncomfortably, but who cares when you are with your love. I took my left hand towards her cheek and I rubbed my hand with her cheek with love, I moved my right hand behind her neck and moved my face towards her. She closed her eyes, and our lips met each other's, I could feel the warmth of her breath and she was totally frozen, she gave herself to me and I was lost in that long kiss which would have broken all the world records if taken into consideration for the world's longest kiss.

Suddenly, it started drizzling. The nature was in a romantic mood too, the rain drops of course could not enter inside the car but created beautiful bubble designs outside the glass of the car. This again worked as a distraction for the people outside, to peek inside the car. Because she did not want me to go out of the car in so much cold and while it's raining, we made ourselves comfortable in the back seat of the car waiting for the rain to stop.

My hand was behind her neck and she was sitting very relaxed as she was a bit tired because of the drive. We were planning for a long drive towards Murthal in next few days. Suddenly she kissed me on my cheeks and when I wanted to kiss her back, she slapped on my cheek with love and started laughing. These types of small mischief make a romantic moment a bit more romantic, and she was best at doing this. I held both her hands tightly with my one hand and kissed her on her cheeks. The random kisses increase the urge to become more romantic with your partner.

I checked my phone and kept silence; she looked at me constantly for a while and then asked "What happen?" I said "I want to relive each and every moment of my life which I had spent with you and that is why I want to record all the memories in my mind, so that I can play them again and again when I am not with you someday".

She became a bit emotional and said "I will always be there with you, don't worry". We both smiled and then went for another kiss, when we kissed each other we used to bend our heads slightly to opposite directions which restrains the nose to come in between while kissing. My hand was on her waist and she unbuttoned the top most button of my shirt, and she kissed my neck. I couldn't think much as in such situation you become spell bound and you go with the flow of what you feel is the best to do. I kissed her neck and I could feel her so close to me that I would never let her go away no matter what happens.

I embraced her in my laps, and she rested her neck on my left arm. I bent slightly downwards and I kissed her forehead, she took her right arm around my neck and smiled at me. I kissed her shoulders and then I kissed her belly.

The rain stopped and her eyes searched for the cell phone and checked the time, "Oh! I am getting late its already 4, she moved to the front seat, adjusted her top and asked me to come to the front seat. I adjusted my shirt and went to the front seat, I hugged her and unwontedly I had to leave.

April 2013

I went to stay at my cousin's house as his family was out of Delhi for some official work and he was alone. The next day I planned to meet Megha at his house, when he leaves for his office. He never knew that I have planned to meet Megha at his house but who cares. He left for his office and I called up Megha to come. Genuinely we were tired of meeting each other at the public places and getting caught by police, or getting afraid of being caught by her relatives. So this was the best thing to spend time with each other and that too when nobody is home.

We were talking to each other on phone while she was on her way to my cousin's home, I was guiding her throughout the way and meanwhile we decided that she is going to make cold coffee and Maggie for our breakfast. She was best at these two things and both Maggie and cold coffee are my all time favorites.

The bell rang and she was there, I opened the door and before anyone of our neighbor see her, she quickly came inside and I closed the door. In our own flat we have to enter like thieves because this society doesn't believe on pre-marital relationships. Finally she was with me, inside the house, all alone and no one to stare us and no one to disturb us.

After a few chit chats on random topics she went towards the kitchen as she knew I was feeling hungry and I dint had breakfast because I wanted to have Maggie and cold coffee made by her. I also joined her in the kitchen to help her in searching and collecting the ingredients and the utensils required. For the first time she was cooking something in front of me and that too for me. I am a big fan of Bollywood and while seeing her cooking a movie scene flash back started running in my mind where hero hugged his girlfriend from behind while she was cooking and the moment was very romantic to see.

To have the same feeling, I went close to her and I put my chin on her left shoulder and both my arms around her waist. She smiled and said, "Babu leave me, *nahi to Maggi kharab ho jaegi.*" and she tried to move a bit, but I asked her to teach me how to make Maggie to divert her mind. She started teaching me how to cook Maggie, and it was totally different from how we make Maggie but I was not at all listening to her as I was lost in the fragrance of her body, I was lost in her shyness of being in my arms, the beauty of her hair falling on her face while she is talking and the moment which was so intense that a man would never try to come out of it. The moment Maggie was ready, She asked, *"Sikh gae na kaise banti hai, ab next time tum banaoge,"* being confused on what to answer I said, "Yes, sure *kyun nahi?*" and then she went on to make the cold coffee.

She poured some milk, coffee, and some sugar into the grinder and then she switched on the power button. After a while, the grinder leaked and the coffee was split very where inside the kitchen and a few drops jumped and settled on her cute face too. Behaving like typical

Indian women, she was worried about the kitchen and I was worried about those coffee drops on her face. She asked be whether today the maid will come to the house to clean and or not to which I replied 'she will come so no need to clean anything but one'. She stared at me and I laughed, her eyes were questioning why I was laughing looking at her and then she asked the expected question, *"Kyu hase ja raha hai kya hua?"*

I asked her if she closes her eyes, I'll tell her what happened, she closed her eyes and I went near her, I kissed her cheek where the coffee drops were spread and I kissed her lips too where a small drop of coffee was trying to hide. She came a bit closer and I gripped her in my hands, I kissed her again and she asked, *"Aaaj achanak se itna pyar kyu aa raha hai."* To which I firmly replied, "*Beta ji pyar nahi aa raha,* a few coffee drops were spread on you face I was just removing them." She smiled and said, "So you found a better way to do this?" Yes I did, I said.

Those few drops of coffee were the tastiest coffee drops of this world and trust me the best thing was that random kiss. We moved towards the room and had our breakfast after that we were just smiling thinking about the last few moments.

She suddenly started laughing, being asked she replied she is missing the day when we both went to Hauz Khas Village, a so-called picnic place of Delhi and a scene got created out there. Let me take you to the flashback.

It was somewhere in the month of march when we both planned to go to Hauz Khas Village, she told me that it was a very nice place according to Kavya and we would feel good if we go there in a cloudy day, by cloudy day we mean the day when the sunrays are not falling directly on us and the rain also doesn't come, but the weather remains cool. Luckily the day when we went to Hauz Khas the day was cloudy, and we really enjoyed the drive towards the Hauz Khas Village.

We entered the Hauz Khas Complex, and headed towards the old buildings which were among the historical monuments. After visiting the Madrasa, pavilions and the mosque we went to the tomb where there was a lake nearby. The tomb has a ground floor near to which the lake was situated and the first floor. Many of the visitors were confined to the first floor only but we went to the ground floor to search for a way to get to the lake. The ground floor has a lane which had various room without the doors but very dark from inside and we could not find a way towards the lake as there was a dead end on that lane. She made a 'u' turn and started to get back to the first floor while I held her hand tight and restrained her from moving upwards.

"Now what?" she said.

"I just want to kiss you, let us get lost in the darkness of this room for a while," I said.

"The guard who is on rounds will see us," she said.

"I'll just take a minute not more than that. I said.

We went inside one of those dark rooms and sneaked in a corner and kissed each other, the darkness grows us wild and we went on kissing each other for few more minutes and then we heard the footsteps of the guard on the round. The guard just crossed our room while coming back and if he catches us inside that room then we would be taken to the police for doing romance at the public place. So she threw a stone to the lake so forcefully that its noise was heard by the guard, no one was allowed to throw the stones inside the lake so the guard thought that someone from the first floor must have done this and he went upstairs running.

As soon as he reached upstairs we also went upstairs but somehow he came to know that we were hiding inside the room in the ground floor and we threw the stone inside the lake, he came to us and asked us to silently move towards the security room where he would take action against us.

We were very much afraid as we never wanted the police to come, so I tried to bribe him. I took a 500 rupee note out of my pocket, looking at the note he became angry and asked for our names and contact numbers of our family. Suddenly someone shouted from the other end, there were some college students who were shouting and misbehaving with the public so the guard went running towards them, we both saw here and there and confirmed that there is no other guard and we ran out of the complex. We sat inside the car, she started it and the guard was back till then, he went on running behind our car but we did not stop till we reached home.

It was a complete memorable visit to the Hauz Khas thinking about which we burst out into laughter sitting at my cousins flat. After a few minutes she looked at her mobile and said, "Sweetheart, I have to leave now as I am already very late!"

She left for her house and I was all alone at my cousin's house replaying the time spent with her again and again.

May 2013

As per the plan which we made on our proposal anniversary, we were on the way to Haveli, a restaurant at Murthal (Haryana). Though it was our first long drive since we were into relationship, we were very much excited to enjoy each and every moment of it. As usual she was driving, I know it was a bit awkward because being a boy I should drive and even though I knew how to drive a car by then, I was reluctant to drive. Just for a formality I asked her, "Shall I drive?" and she nodded her head in yes. Being a girl she always wanted her man to be strong enough in every possible thing, I shifted to the driver's side and started driving.

She switched on the FM and we were totally lost in those romantic songs and were singing along with the track as loud as possible. She was worried about my driving but I was carefree because I knew if I am stuck somewhere and if I couldn't drive, she will. Looking at the speed she said "If you will keep driving so slowly we will reach Haveli by tomorrow", I changed the gear and started driving as fast as I could and it drove us wild.

It was a journey of almost one hour and half an hour was already passed when the sun become a bit angry on us and the Delhi FM could no more provide us the Songs as we were out of Delhi by then. As we know the phone rings only when we are with our partner and that too when we are in roaming, our phone started ringing but we did not care as the calls were not from our home.

Looking for some beautiful songs she connected the aux cable to my phone and started shuffling the songs. Meanwhile my eyes moved to the rear view mirror when

I noticed that a Van was trying to take over our car and they slowed down the speed when they were parallel to us. The guy next to the driver on the front seat started peaking out his head from the side window of the van and did some vulgar gestures towards us. With no offence this was quite usual in Haryana, where people are drunk and they commit crime.

Megha asked me to not to look at them and try to speed up the car as if we slow down they might harm us. Though it was not a empty road, there is was a lot of traffic too, but today nobody is there to save as no one likes to get into someone else's matter. I increased the speed of the car and after a few kilometers we couldn't see they, may be they stopped somewhere or they changed their way. We relaxed and I started driving to the normal speed once again. We both were afraid and I asked her to check how many kilometers we were away from Haveli.

"It's just 10 kms away," she said and the van was back again with a high speed. I sped up my car and I drove it like a racing car, they over took us and slowed down their speed and did let us go ahead of them. I asked her to call the police, she looked up for her phone which showed battery low and shut down. She started searching my phone, which wasn't showing the network. Oh my god! All the problems have to come at the same time she said.

There comes a check point, I slowed down my car and was wondering if police is there, so that I can complaint to them about the van. The van driver also slowed down being afraid of the police and he took his van behind a truck and let us go ahead. While moving closer to the barricades I noticed there was not a single policeman and we had to again speed up the car. I never drove the car so fast and trust me my legs are hurting I said to her.

She was worried about me, and I was worried about her. The van had at least 5 – 6 people in it and I did not have any choice except to keep driving and did not let them over take us again. The Van driver was not afraid of anything on the road, as he was drunk too. He tried to overtake us again, from the left side. I just let him come parallel to us and then I speeded up my car and moved my car towards a slight left, the van driver also took his van a slight left where the van lost its balance and struck a tree on the left side.

We knew the people inside the van were hurt badly but we did not stop, as if any one of them calls up few more people from his known, we would have held responsible for their accident and the things would have taken a more serious situation. We wanted to see those bastard, I took my car reverse, went parallel to the van and through the gestures the driver was asking me to help him out of the van, he was bleeding.

I realized, a few minutes back he was the person because of whom Megha was very much afraid, and what if his van wouldn't have met that accident, if they would have been able to stop us, would they spare us. Megha asked me to start the car and get back to the home, looking at the driver I raised my middle figure in front of him and drove the car toward Haveli.

We reached Haveli and made over selves comfortable on the table for two. My sweet heart was not in any mood to have anything that time; she was very much frustrated and angry. I gently asked her to order something to eat but she said she is not in mood to order anything. I took the menu and keep on looking for the things to order, but as usual I was not at all able to decide what to order,

I looked at her, she was busy in checking her phone. I again tried to look for something of her choice and my choice too, but again I couldn't find anything which we both may like. She looked at me and snatched the menu, "You can never order anything I know, and I'll have to help you". Just like a perfect sweetheart she then ordered something which we both liked "the red chilli paratha and the green chilli paratha with some daal and butter roti".

The order would take 15 – 20 minutes Ma'am, the waiter said. We were already very late because of those idiots and Megha was still very much worried and frustrated. I moved toward the rest room and while going there I saw a small child in the dress of a waiter, he was the child of the waitress sitting in the reception. I just asked the waitress to help me in making Megha smile. She wondered how I would do that, I then asked her to send her child with me for a few minutes and she agreed. I went to the child, handed him over a chocolate and I asked him to come to my table when I went back to my seat. He smiled at me and agreed to do what I wanted him to.

I came back to the seat and asked Megha about the status of our order, she said it will be there in 5 minutes. That small child came to her with a red rose, he said, "I love you didi and CK also loves you a lot, please *apna* mood *thik kallo...*"

Megha excepted the flower and smiled at him, she asked him who told her to do so, and the child pointed out his figure at me. She kissed the child on his cheek and said, "CK *ko bhi meri taraf se ek kissi de dena.*" The child came to me and kissed on my cheek and said, "Bhaiya, *aap mujhe ek aur chocolate doge?*" I smiled at him and gave him one more chocolate which I kept for Megha.

Her mood was okay now, and she was happy that at last I was somehow able to make her smile, the lunch arrived, and we had those chilli parathas and moved back to the car. This time I am going to drive, she said sitting on the driver's seat. I smiled and we started back to Delhi. While going back to Delhi, we saw the same van was surrounded by the PCR and Ambulance, on the other side of the road. A man was passing by our car, I asked Megha to stop the car and asked that man, "*Kya hua* uncle?" He said, "They met an accident, may be they were drunk and all were badly hurt." Megha started the car, she looked at me and we both smiled at each other.

We reached home, but thereafter we never talked to each other about that matter, and we never went to Haveli after that, of course the urge to go for a long drive took us to the Ambience Mall, Gurgaon after few days of that scene. But this time nothing serious happened except her car's tyre got punctured and I we had to take a risk to hand over the keys to a mechanic nearby to get that tyre fixed till we come back from our shopping, which he did genuinely and we were back home safely.

July 2013 (A Lie)

I was at my home town enjoying the vacations after the completion of my MBA, Megha and I talked to each other for the whole day. And by whole day I mean whenever we were free and no one was around us to notice us while we are talking to each other. One day she was out with her friends, I called her up and during the conversation I asked whether she has a plan to booze with her friends that day. She replied that she has no plans of getting drunk and why am I asking this question to her, as I never asked her this question before.

I was confused and I don't know why, but it was my sixth sense which was telling me that she is going to booze that day. Although she never did anything which I did not liked and if she wanted to do such thing she informs me before doing it, so if she would have had a plan then she must have told me. Because I never wanted her to get indulged in such things, I always tried to keep her away from those things. I never booze, and never did I want her to. I hanged up the call as my mom saw me talking to someone from last half an hour, after few hours Megha called me back and again I asked her whether she is drunk, but the reply was negative. I had a strong feeling that she is surely drunk but if I was feeling, it doesn't mean that she really is, so I did not say anything to her except few words, "I trust you and I know you will never break it."

The next day while she was on the way to her home from the college, she said, "I want to tell you something but you will have to promise that you will not get angry on me."

I said, "Okay I'll will not."

She said, "You were right, I was drunk yesterday, earlier when you asked I didn't had any plan to booze but when I was offered the drink by my friend I did not inform you because you would have stopped me from boozing." She did not reveal that truth yesterday because she thought I would get angry on her and she knew when I get angry I'll either shout on her or would not talk to her, in both cases we both get hurt.

My reaction was blank, I became angry because she was drunk and more than that she lied to me for the first time in the last 4 years of the relationship and I hated this, I never wanted her to lie as I never did and when you start lying the trust in the relationship gets finished. I disconnected the call and sent her a message that I will not talk to her till she is sorry for what she did and she promises me that she will never drink with her friends hereafter.

She was sorry for what she did, she knew that I was loyal in the relationship and I never lied to her. I always shared each and everything to her irrespective of what her reaction is going to be. She understood the level of pain I may be going through when she lied to me, but somehow she did not wanted to promise that she will not booze when she is with her friends, because according to her boozing with the friends occasionally was not a crime and every one does that and if you say no to a friend they would laugh on you and say, "Come on you are mature enough to take your decisions and you are capable enough to control yourself when you are drunk." and it is a trend to drink with friends when you are out with them.

But according to me if you say no to a friend it doesn't mean that you are behaving kiddishly, or you are showing them that you are afraid of something, it means that more than anything else you respect your family values, you respect you religion if it doesn't allow you to booze, you respect the trust of your partner on you and more than that you respect yourself that you need not do something which reduces your self-respect just to show it to others that you are big enough to booze, I mean who does that, if you booze it doesn't mean you have grown older, does it build up your image if you drink. You should always do what is right for you.

You never realize what you are going to do when you are drunk and after a few occasions you eventually start doing it regularly, and being her love I would never let her do something which will harm her or our relationship, and never will I do anything which would harm me and our relationship either. After a long argument she agreed and she realized what I was trying to make her understand, she was too concerned about what if I start boozing. Then after thinking for few seconds she said I will promise that I'll never drink with my friends but on one condition, the condition that you will also never booze when you are with your friends, I agreed as I knew I'll never do.

She promised me that she will never booze when she is with her friends. Of course, she was allowed to drink when she is with her family and relatives as it is very rare.

I knew her mood was off, but when you are into a relationship, you have to give up few bad things which your partner wants you to, for your good and when it was for her good, I had to make her promise.

July 2014 (Unedited Romance)

I was waiting for her at my home, where I had shifted a few months back, since I had started my own business. I was staying alone now as I wanted to make myself independent. Though Mamaji and Mamiji felt very unhappy to let me go from their house, I had made my mind and they had no choice left.

She has been here many times before but I don't know why today I felt like this day is special and I should enjoy each and every moment of this day. Maybe I was feeling this way as we were meeting each other after almost a month and I was emotional, but my sixth sense always sensed something unusual. I was busy thinking why I am feeling very uncomfortable and so worried, I rarely feel that way. Meanwhile, she was there at the door.

I opened the door and let her in. I was quiet as some thoughts were still running somewhere inside my head. I did not pay much attention to her dress, and asked her to sit. She asked me where I was lost, to which I replied, "I don't know but I am feeling very negative, some negative thoughts about our relationships are running in my head and I don't want them to come out." To change the topic I asked whether she has had her breakfast or not.

She said she has had her breakfast and asked me whether I had eaten. To which I replied, "When I am waiting for you I never feel hungry for food," and I smiled.

"What do you mean by hungry for food? What else do you feel hungry for?"

Nothing, I just wanted to say I was not feeling hungry, but now when you are talking about the food I have started feeling hungry. I asked her to cook something for me as she used to tell me that she is a very good cook. After a few ifs and buts she finally agreed to cook something for me, when she asked me what I would like to have I opted for 'Red Chili Paratha', my favorite.

She moved to the kitchen and I was standing beside her; she took out plate and put some flour and then poured some water into it. I was looking at her, and trust me girls hate this when you stare at them. She asked me what I was looking for.

"Only three people in a man's life cooks in the kitchen of his house. One is his mom, another is his sister and the third one is his Love. I am very happy that that third person is you and the dream to see you cooking at my home and my kitchen is fulfilled today." She smiled and tried to manage her hair falling on her eyes but she could not as her fingers were wet and full of flour, so I helped her hair behind her ear. I kissed her and we both smiled at each other.

I went back to the room to check my phone and play some romantic songs on the TV, and after a few minutes she came inside the room and said "Parathe ready!"

I had a look at the parathas made by her, they were over-baked, and a lot of ghee applied on them. She helped me with few bites and I loved the way she fed me. After a few bites she asked me how the taste was I responded "They are not better than what mom makes, but they are certainly better then all those dishes which you made me try on my last birthday when we went to Kingdom of Dreams!"

She smiled and said, "Those were traditional dishes, after all we rarely get to eat the dishes of almost all the states at one single place and I enjoyed trying those dishes. But you don't change the topic, please say the parathas were tasty and that I am a good cook,"

I knew there is no way out. "They are not tasty, they are very tasty!" She was happy to listen to this, after all a girl is hungry for praise.

She said, "I am happy that you think about me so much; you care and love me so much, I am glad that I have you in my life and I pray we always remain together forever." A tear of happiness rolled down from her eyes, she smiled and said, "I was very happy when you made my last birthday special by giving me birthday surprise which I never thought you will do."

"I did nothing much, it was just that you wanted all your cousins, your school and college friends to be at one place with you and me and I called them up to plan a surprise and the plan did work out."

Few of her friends did not turn up but those who came were awesome people, her college friends Riya, Yamini and Nishika were the best people I have ever met with. I realized how good her friends circle is, and her real sis Kavya also joined us there. All I did is brought her inside the domino's blind folded to the table where everyone who was unexpected by her was sitting in front of her when she opened up her eyes. Then we had a cake cutting and then the girls were busy taking selfies.

"After all a different thing happened that day, Yamini took few pictures of us without letting us know and this was the first time in 5 years of relationship when we got a photograph clicked in which we both were together."

Strange but true, we have never got a photograph clicked together and this year everything happened very differently, I celebrated her birthday differently, I met her friends which I never did in last 5 years, I taught her the subjects of MBA during her exams, and she cooked the food at my home. Thinking all this made me realize that not only the intuition that this day is going to be special the whole year has been very special for me and her too.

I showed her the pictures which Yamini clicked, and then she went on to lift the guitar which was kept beside the bed. The guitar was not mine; it was of my cousin Nitesh who recently joined the guitar classes. She unzipped the cover and asked me to take a few clicks of her with that guitar and then asked me to learn guitar so that I could play a song for her next time when she comes at my home. I asked her if she would also like to join the guitar classes with me like the salsa classes but she did not have time because of her studies.

Suddenly, I again started feeling very uneasy, negative thoughts were ruining my mood again. I was feeling like we were going to face some trouble in our relationship and because of it I was lost thinking more and more about it, suddenly she came close to me and asked, "Are you okay sweet heart?"

"Yes, I am okay," I replied smiling.

She was looking very pretty and I just wanted to kiss her, I went close to her and touched her cheeks with my hand, she closed her eyes and I went ahead to kiss her. The lips got locked and we were lost in each other, that sweet taste of her kiss and the mesmerizing smell of her body took me to the cloud nine. Where we both were alone with each other and no one was around to look at us. I bent her slightly on my left arm and carried on the kiss which I never wanted to end.

She was in my control and I was in hers, I let her hair loose by removing her hair clip and was drawing imaginary lines in her hair., I rubbed my nose against her and smiled. Her eyes became deep and dark, they were asking me to hold her tightly. My right hand automatically tried to lift her top and made her free from those cotton-made locks which were not required between us. The shirt of mine got unbuttoned like I never had it on my body, the darkness of the room helped us very well but shyness is a girl's ornament and she was with me in the square room with no boundaries between us.

We both were deeply and madly in each other's arms, and there was no point to stop. I kissed her again and her nails were scratching my back but they were doing their task. I kissed her arms, which made me feel her fragrance deeply; I wanted to swim in her deep innocent eyes, the love was intense and more intense was our trust in each other. She gripped me and allowed me to kiss her legs, and she was feeling touchy when I went on to kiss her belly.

I wanted to feel her heartbeat and by getting my ear close to heart I tried to listen to her beats getting faster. She was now all over me, we were two bodies and one soul and there is always a point to connect these; we had no regrets and no complaints, the only thing was love and I was inside her. I could see the pain in her eyes but that pain was just a part of our body. The soul in the two bodies were connected and remained connected for a while, till the strength of getting against the nature prevailed, but it seemed to be happening and we were there, she felt me inside her each and every moment.

After a few minutes…

"Jaan, I have to go, I don't know when we felt asleep and it's too late. Mom's call is about to come," she said.

"Hang on! Can't you tell your mom that you are going to live with me here forever, or I would have to tell your family that I am going to marry your daughter and she is mine now?"

"And they are going to say, oh! We are so glad, go ahead, marry her, take her to your home and they would bless us. Now would you please let me dress up and go home?"

"Okay! *Abhi jaane de raha hu*, but remember very soon you are going to be with me permanently and forever."

She looked for her accessories and dressed up. She applied her lip gloss and fixed her hair, she was all set to go, I stopped her and said, "I will miss you Jaan."

She smiled and said, "Stop behaving like a child, I am here in Delhi only, I am not going out of Delhi."

We had a good bye kiss and then I was all alone at my home, recollecting those awesome moments which we had just spent with each other. I and she, she and I, we were now ours, and that removed the fear of mine, the feeling that we are going to face some trouble in our relationship. This was the day when I was hers and she was mine, and we were in a emotional contract of being with each other forever and we had no chance for the breach of this contract.

The day was special and will always remain special. The intuition which kept made me awake and alert to enjoy and live each and every moment of today made me feel awesome, and I thanked god from deep down of my heart that he had given the best gift of my life to me and that gift was Megha.

End of It

It was 12:13 pm, Tuesday morning on 5th August 2014, when we met happily for the last time. She didn't have her college that day, and I was waiting for her at the food court in the City centre mall, Rohini. She was late as always and me, constantly calling her to ask where she had reached. I got very frustrated because of her habit to coming late, but when I saw her as usual everything I became calm. There she is… soft, silky, straight hair, deep and beautiful eyes, wearing her favorite sky blue top and carrying a heart-shaped hand bag. Sitting in front of me, with her butterfly smile she asked, "*Gussa hai*?"

"No, I just forget everything when I see you!" I said. Thinking on back of my mind, "You come late, I wait for you, every second waiting for you is like an hour for me sweetheart, and this makes me impatient to see you!" "What would you like to have JAAN?" I said. "Nothing, I have done breakfast but you have not, so can I get something for you?" she replied. "Umm, okay let me order white pasta for both of us. But you don't like white pasta," she said remembering my preference for red pasta. But I told her, "I like everything which you like and that's where my happiness lies sweetheart…"

"So! When we are going to meet next?" I asked.

"You are always in a hurry to meet me, why so?" she replied.

"The moment I separate from you I start waiting for the next meet," I replied.

I held her hand and we both smiled at each other, and the pasta arrived.

We ate lunch and made small talk. Suddenly she looked up at me and said, "It's already 2 o'clock sweetheart and I have to leave now."

We both then went to her car and I couldn't go away from her, so I got inside her car and asked her to spend few more minutes with me. I was driving and I don't know why I started it…

We both started fighting about small things for the last 3 nights and I was not able to sleep because of it, I cry till my eyes could handle it no more, can we discuss it today so that it's finally over and we don't have to fight anymore, I said.

"Not now, I am not in any mood to discuss it and I have to go home, will discuss about this over the phone…" she replied. "We are not able to solve it on the phone, the fight always increases and we end up disconnecting the phone and spoiling each other's moods. Let's discuss it and solve it now and forever. I cannot cry every night and think about it for the whole day; I will not let you go till we solve everything which is screwing up our relationship," I said.

She refused to discuss about those things and I tried to force her. She moved her head and face to the opposite side and I forced her to look at me again and again. She started her car to go home but I switched it off and took out the keys. She asked me for the keys and I did not gave it to her. In anger I said I will not let you go till you solve these problems right now and she forcefully snatched the car keys and started the engine once again. We both were stubborn and we both stuck to our decision., The arguments took a very serious form and they became very aggressive within a few minutes. Neither did she wanted to change her decision, nor did I. We both were quarrelling like enemies and it became so serious which we never expected.

After an hour I gave up because she started crying, she did not want me to discuss the reasons for which we were fighting every night because according to her those reasons were silly. She got very angry with me because of my bad behavior and she could only say, "Listen it's over! I gave you many chances but you always misbehave in public places, and I hate you for this. Goodbye there is no need to talk to me ever. Don't call me!" She left me in the pain again.

Does it really matter whether we discuss these things at our home, over the phone or in a closed car parked in a public place; the important thing is our relationship and to save it we cannot see the time and place, we just want to solve it and why we cannot discuss those things sitting inside a car if we can have a discussion on any other topic like the next date with her or the plan for shopping.

The only thing I could do is call her repeatedly but she hung up the phone saying don't call me I'll never ever talk to you.

I went home, tried to call her several times regretting for what I had done and blaming myself for ruining it once again. A happy day turned into a sad day and I was banging my head on the walls of my house, abusing myself and having pity on myself for once again breaking the promise which I had made to her. I tried to call and message her again and again but it did not give me anything except a silence from her side. I never thought this thing could hurt her so much and our relationship would be at stake.

I did not have my dinner that day, was thinking about those moments again and again and I wished if I could go to the past and stop myself from doing this, I tried to sleep but I couldn't as my pillow was wet because of the continuous tears falling from my eyes. I thought the next day would give me a better solution for convincing her to talk to me and with that hope I was awake all night.

I said I love her
I said I like her
But she thinks it is a joke…
I like her behavior
I like her character
But she believes it is an irony…
I like her nearness
I like her charm
But she assumes it is a mischief…
I understand her feelings
I understand her breathings
But she let it to be a cheating…
I keep her loving
I keep her dreaming
But when it breaks it raining, raining and raining…

06th August, 2014

Do I need to see a psychiatrist?

I was awake the whole night and I was waiting for her call at 8:30am. This was the time when she is usually on the way to her college and she calls me up daily at this time. With every second the clock moved towards 8:30, my heart started beating faster and faster. I was not afraid of her reaction when she called me up, but I was afraid of losing her. The clock strike 8:30 and my eyes moved towards my mobile, every second of her delay multiplied my fear that she was now very angry with me and she was not going to forgive me this time. I did not get any call from her for next 5 minutes. I convinced myself that she has not called me because she might be late for the college today so she would call me as soon as she started driving towards the college.

It was 8:45, no call from her. I was unlocking the mobile screen again and again to check whether the network was there or not. But now I could not wait any longer, I called her; she did not pick up the call. I tried it once again, then she sent a busy tone. Maybe she was not going to college today that is why she is not receiving the calls, I convinced myself.

In the afternoon I tried calling her again and again she disconnected the call saying she did not want to talk to me and sent me a message saying that I should not call her. I checked her Whatsapp status where she wrote, “Frustrated”. She wasn’t online since last night, I sent her a message that I want to talk to her and I promised I would listen to her and she could dump all her anger on me. It was my mistake and I had to convince her, so she somehow agreed to talk to me in the evening.

After a long wait I got a call from her at 11pm in the night. I was silent when I received the call and she was very angry with me. I thought I would be able to convince her and I tried with the word 'Sorry', to which she replied, "Do you have something new, every time you make the mistake and then say sorry... does sorry solves everything?"

I did not have words because I knew nothing was going to work out here and I had never seen her getting so angry so I asked her to just think about what my life would be without her and forgive me. I asked her to think about those beautiful moments we shared together and come back. I asked her to share what was on her mind with me and to not let her anger to come in between us. After a pause she replied, "Look, I will get back into the relationship but on one condition..." I took a breath of relief and I said, "Tell me, I would do anything to bring you back..."

According to her I needed to see a psychiatrist, because I behave very badly when I am angry. I was taking every small argument seriously because of which I quarrel with her and I am behaving very different in these days, Even the lack of sleep and the insecurity about the relationship supported her suggestion, she also said she would only get into the relationship if I consulted a psychiatrist.

I was damn worried about all of the things which she said. I could not prove anything as I knew these things were true and then I came up with a solution. I said, my best friend Vatsala from IIPM is a psychologist and we will have a discussion about my problems with her, if she suggests further counselling we will definitely go to the psychiatrist if required.

She agreed to have a conversation with Vatsala over conference call and I asked Vatsala to come into the call for the discussion. We shared the whole situation with Vatsala; the small arguments about on which we fought, my bad behavior with Megha and about my current situation of not being able to sleep. I was also becoming over expressive and emotional about everything. After analyzing all those things, Vatsala came to the conclusion that due to over thinking on useless things suppressed anger had developed in me and because of which I was not behaving well. She said currently I do not need to see a psychiatrist as it was just anger management which I need to learn and she provided me with few tips on anger management.

Megha however did not seem to be convinced until Vatsala wanted to talk to her privately and then they both came up with a solution that Megha would allow me 2 months to learn to control my anger, to improve my behavior and during these 2 months she would just be my friend, not a girlfriend.

I felt very alone. But I somehow convinced myself that Megha wants me to become better than what I am and even Vatsala had my best interests at heart. So I equipped myself to become a better person to learn and control my anger. I felt very ashamed when I recollected the moments in which I was shouting at Megha and I promised myself to become a good man for her, like I was when we had started the relationship way back in 2009.

We both were together but we were not. We both were talking to each other but we were not like we used to. I knew that we both loved each other more than anyone else in this world but we were just friends for now. We both wanted to speak up a lot of things but we were silent on everything now. I was finding this time very difficult as I was on my best behavior and my beloved girlfriend did not seem to reciprocate. It hurt me tremendously when she did not respond to my overtures of '**I Love You!**' I was just trying to settle down everything and get the relationship back to the track by doing every possible thing I could do and she was behaving as badly as she could just to analyze the changes in me. When I used to call her up and share all the things in my mind she listened to me but it seemed like she was not really interested in talking to me and always wanted to end the conversation. I always used to get angry with her behavior with me but because I couldn't show her my anger, I too used the technique to disconnect the call so that I could cool down.

I started thinking that she did not want to get back into the relationship. I was upset and my thoughts were muddled and confusing, even to me. It was all a blur and I told myself, "*She knows that I can't live without her, that is why she wants me to learn to live without talking to her, without sharing the things to her, without meeting her and just be her friend till she says she is ready for the relationship.*" Now because of all this I was now more worried, more frustrated, and more insecure than ever. And this once again fuelled the vicious cycle of anger within me and I started to sense the anger building in me. But on the other hand she might be thinking that her awkward behavior will teach me a lesson.

Still I tried to control my anger, and I told her that I am doing my best to control my anger but according to her there were no changes in me. I wondered I could end my anger instead of controlling it. Everyone in this damn world knows anger cannot be ended, you can only control it and I was trying my best to control it.

I tried to meet her two times in those two month even when she refused to meet me, but both the times I drove towards her college and met her to convince her that I am trying my best and I am feeling the changes in me. But this always increased her frustration towards me and she ended up shouting at me to leave her alone and not to try to meet her again without her consent.

Those 2 months which were equal to 2 years with her and without her. Life seems so pathetic. That time without her made me weak, and I was damn depressed. I lost interest in my business, and I isolated myself. I was feeling that I had somehow controlled my anger as I believed that I was behaving well. So again I went to her college to meet her when the 2 months' time was over, just to convince her that I had changed and to come back to me now.

When I reached her college she was about to leave for her home, I asked her to meet me at Rithala Metro Station as she had to drop her friend there. I reached Rithala before her and I waited for her there, I prayed to God to bring her back to me and I promised him that I will never misbehave with her again. She came and I went inside her car, she did not want to talk so she kept mum. I asked her whether she is feeling the changes in me or not, to which she replied that I have not changed a bit and coming to meet her again and again, she hated me for this.

I told her how I was feeling without her, how I am spending all my time in improving myself but her negligence towards me is killing me. I was controlling my anger every time and I never got angry on her since last two months, but according to her I was just controlling my anger and I should learn not to become angry which was not at all possible. She said, "Listen I never wanted you to do this and I just wanted you to come to meet me only when I want you too, because according to me we are just friends and we would have been friends till you learn how to behave, I am not going to talk to you anymore and you have not changed a bit, our friendship is over!"

I thought I should call Vatsala and again have a conversation with her in front of Megha, so that things can be solved, but she did not wanted to talk to anyone and left me alone once again. May be she wanted to see more changes in me, because of course a true lover cannot live without you and she might not have been able to, but for my better she had to do this, she had to hurt me and break that friendship at that point and I was all over from inside. She drove back to home crying and in anger and I sat on my bike to try to regain my senses. I did not knew what all is going in her head and I did not knew what is going to happen next, but as of now we both were separated again and the last hope which was our friendship also ended.

I requested Vatsala to talk to her and try to solve the things. After a conversation with Megha, Vatsala said that she had made up her mind to end this. Maybe you have not changed, maybe she is not able to see the changes, or maybe she doesn't want to see the changes. This shattered me from inside, I lost all my hope to bring her back as she was not replying to my phone calls and messages. I was crying sitting alone in my home. It was just a misunderstanding between us, which did not get cleared up and ended the relationship between us for a while. The things which could not be solved should be left un- discussed and this was the lesson I learned when she broke up with me.

I kept wondering whole night will she come back?

October 2014

Being alone and depressed, I was just wondering if there was anything which could help me get her back. I got an idea, I searched for her college friend Riya on FB and asked for her phone number as she seemed to be the most trustworthy person who could convince Megha for what I wanted her to. I called her up, explained everything to her. I told Riya about all of the things which created the misunderstanding between Megha and me, and the mistakes which I committed and her behavior towards me.

She said Megha had never discussed anything about her personal life with any of her friends in the college. She did not wanted to get into it, but because I was sad and I looked convincing to her, she was ready to help me out. She had a conversation with Yamini and Nishika and it took us about a week to make up a plan on how to convince Megha to get back into the relationship.

Meanwhile my Mom came to Delhi, to stay with me for a month and I was happy that she was here with me when I was all alone and sad. mom knew about me being in a relationship with Megha and she always used to say that she wants to meet Megha but I was shy and I always said, "Mom I don't have any girlfriend..."

Before Riya, Yamini and Nishika could convince Megha I thought if I asked my Mom to do this for me, there might be better chances to bring her back into my life.

I called up Megha and told her that my mom wanted to meet her; somehow she agreed to come home and meet my mom. I came to my mom and I don't know why but suddenly I started crying in front of her, she got worried and asked me the reason for being so sad and I then explained her everything. She became very angry because of what I did with Megha and she wanted me to call her and ask her to meet my mom, which I had already did. Then I called up Riya and informed her that my mom had called Megha at my home and she would take care of everything and they can now relax.

I was once again in a tense and nervous state. There were so many thoughts running around in my head and I was waiting for the next morning eagerly now. I wanted it to come early but late, I was happy but afraid. I dint knew what was going to happen tomorrow; I did not know whether she would agree to be back in the relationship or not. I wondered, "*Will my mom convince her for me or she will ask her to leave me. Will my mom like her or not...*" These questions kept hitting my head hard for the whole night. I was so happy that I was smiling that my mom agreed to talk to her but tears were coming out of my eyes because I was afraid of losing her again. I could not sleep the whole night as I was wondering what will be the reaction of Megha when she confronts my mom. I wondered, "*Will she complain to my mom about me, will she tell her that I slapped her once and I shouted on her in a public place, after listening to her will my mom ask me to leave her alone as I committed all those mistakes which were un acceptable...*"

I dint knew whether I slept that night or not, but the morning arrived and she was going to be here at 8:30 today. She called me up and said she that she would be there in few minutes; I went to my mom into the kitchen and requested her to somehow convince Megha for me. She said she will try her best.

Megha entered my house; she wished my mom and then started the discussion on what we were waiting for. My mom asked her the reason for the breakup to which she replied that because of my bad behavior in a public place that too, and my possessive nature she did not want to be with me. She said she loves me and my nature but when I get angry I never behave properly. She even told my mom that I slapped her once and even after that we had many fights at the public places. She explained her about the last instance where we had fight and even then I did not change myself.

After listening to her my mom became very angry on me and she said if she would have been Megha's mom she would have never allowed her to talk to me hereafter but still If I am sorry for what I had done and if I promise to take care and love Megha always and will never misbehave and get angry on her, then she would ask Megha to talk to me.

I was sorry for what I did; I tried my level best to change myself, and I was damn worried to lose her. Even if my mom would have asked me to cut my neck and place it in Megha's feet I would have done that, I agreed with my mom and I promised that I would never commit those mistakes again. Megha smiled at my Mom and then at me and she was back into the relationship again. My mom also asked Megha to call her if I misbehave with her hereafter.

Megha was very comfortable with my mom, they were so busy in their conversation like they knew each other from years. I was isolated and felt like they had nothing to do with me. I never knew that situation would turn around so easily and they would be so comfortable with each other within an hour. I was feeling like my mom was Megha's mom and I was Megha's husband who came to live at Megha's house and I had no importance of mine at her house. After all, she was mine again and we all were happy, my mom, me, Megha and my life.

Megha was about to leave, but I did not wanted her to. My sixth sense informed me that if Megha goes to the college today, her friends would tell her that we were making a plan to convince her and it was not the time when I should tell her that I was talking to her friends to makeup a plan to convince her. Because I knew listening to this she will get angry on me and everything will be ruined once again. I asked her to not to go to college that day and how about enjoying the day out with each other somewhere. But she said she had an important class and she have to go to college anyhow.

I wanted to stop her but I couldn't as if I had then she would have again become angry on me. She left for her college and I went to my office hoping everything will be fine. But if life would have been so simple then we would have never faced so many problems and the upcoming one again.

She called me when her classes were over and she was very angry, she asked me to come and meet her and I had to hurriedly leave my office to meet her. I knew it's her friends who had ruined the things for me again. Those who once promised me to help me in solving everything have created the problems for me. She was very angry knowing that I have told her friends about our breakup and the problems which were going on in our relationship which she never wanted to share with them. She also said that I have plotted my mom to convince her otherwise my mom never wanted to meet her. When I insisted her to tell me the name of the person who has told her about these things she said it was Mathur who has told her everything.

Again a misunderstanding and I was damn angry on Mathur for doing this, if I would have been the king of this country, I would have sentenced Mathur to be hanged till death for doing this. She never knew anything about me and Megha and she had no rights to ruin a relationship when she does not know anything about us. I asked Megha to forget whatever they said to her, I asked her to just trust me and stop thinking too much. I told her that yes I was talking to her friends to make a plan to bring her back into the relationship but I haven't plotted my mom for this, it was just that I cried in front of my mom and she asked me about the matter and she herself wanted to meet her and then I asked my mom to convince her for me.

But my luck was against me and she was not at all listening to me, she jumped to the conclusion that I lied to her that my mom wanted to meet her which she really did. She also thought that I was playing around with her emotions to bring her back. Those few friends of her who came into her life a few months back were now trustworthy for her and I was a liar. I never knew my life would become so pathetic that the person who trusted me more than she trusts herself now thinks I was wrong.

She was so much frustrated that she said she wanted to end this forever and she doesn't want to come back into the relationship. She apologized to my mom for changing her decision and my mom knew that Megha has lost her trust on me and there was no point in keeping that relationship anymore. She asked me to leave her alone and try to live without her.

I have tried everything which I could, and I was left with no hope, but I was angry with Riya because if she would not have told Mathur about whatever happened, then Megha would have not broken up with me again. I called her up and asked her to meet me in front of all of them (Yamini, Mathur and Nishika). She agreed to meet me the next day and I went to her college to meet all of them.

We all gathered in the college canteen and I asked them the reason behind telling Megha about our plans, to which Riya replied that she just shared everything with Mathur which she could not do earlier, and Mathur thought that I was really plotting everyone to convince Megha and that is why she informed Megha about everything. Mathur's misunderstanding was now Megha's misunderstanding and Mathur has ruined everything.

I burst out crying in front of them and when I narrated them the whole story on how much we loved each other, they realized that by mistake they have ruined a relationship which was far better than all other relationships and they agreed to talk to Megha about this and make her understand that this is mere a misunderstanding, and everything which I had done so far was just to bring her back.

Megha was called up there and all her friends explained her about the misunderstandings which have created havoc in our life, but Megha kept silence, her silence kills me and it was. After all the emotional discussions she said, "May be there were a lot of misunderstandings which ruined our relationship but the main thing is your nature and behavior, I am ready to be you friend and if you promise to change yourself then I'll be back into your life as your girlfriend and this will be your last chance."

I hugged her and I promised her that I'll never repeat those mistakes again and I will make myself better than before. My life was just like a pendulum now, she comes back gives me happiness for few moments and then goes away and fill my eyes with tears. It was a war between me and my luck, every time my luck took her away from me I somehow brought her back, every time my luck gave me a kick, I gathered all my energy and fought back.

I was happy that she was back as a friend in my life, but I was sad because she was not the same anymore. She already has lost trust in me and I had nothing to do to develop that trust again except to give time to the things to heal on their own. I came back home with a new hope that I will change myself and make myself a better man to get her back into my life.

Things become bad, then worst but they eventually become better and I hope this time it's going to be better. My life has nothing more important than her and I knew what she meant to me, Mom didn't knew that I have met Megha again and even she did not wanted me to meet her again but I had to tell my mom about it and I told my mom everything. Mom did not say anything about me and Megha and then she informed me about her plan to go to Vrindavan the next day.

03rd October, 2014

We were at Bankey Bihari temple, everyone folded their hands in front of the God of Love, Lord Krishna. I jumped off few people and tried to go closest to the Krishna, I went near his ears and said, "You are the God of Love, I know I have committed many mistakes while I was in relationship but now I want you to help me get her back, I am trying to make myself a better man for her and you are going to help me in doing so. Bring her back for me I promise ill come to see you within next month and I'll always be your follower if you do this."

When we went to Iskon temple, I kept myself busy in chanting Hare Rama Hare Krishna with the foreigners who used to chant mantras daily, I had never been so religious and seeing this my mom and dad got surprised that I am chanting the mantras which I never do. This was the power of Love, the fear of losing showed me the way to god, had anyone told me that you have to do these chants for the whole day without having food and water; I would have done that to get her back.

I have never shown so much interest in god and I have never visited to so many temples in a single day which I did that day. At every temple I went, I had only one line to say to god, "I Love her and I want her back, I trust you and I promise ill never hurt her, please bring her back in my life."

When I visited an old Yamuna Temple, there was an old lady sitting just outside the temple, unlike others she was not bagging, she was busy in chanting Krishna, Krishna, Hare Krishna, and when I looked at her she looked very mysterious yet poor and weak. Her face expressed her age being in 70's and her health showed how poor she was. My subconscious mind asked me to go to her, touch her feet and ask her for her blessings and give her some money so that she could get some food for herself. But eventually my Dad and my Mamaji went to her, they touched her feet and gave her some money.

She looked at me continuously and I felt she wanted to say something to me but I thought if I go close to her I would burst out crying thinking about my relationship and asking for her blessing to settle down everything. Meanwhile my cousin asked me to get out of there as we were getting late so I had to leave without having a conversation with that lady. For the whole day her face kept on flashing in my eye and I felt like she was calling me to say something to me but I had no chance to go to her again as we had to go to Agra the very next day.

The short night passed away very easily as I was lost in my thoughts where I was wondering things could get worst within no time, there was a day few years back when I came to Vrindavan and I asked Lord Krishna that I am enjoying a very happy life I want you to keep blessing me and my girlfriend and today was the day when I prayed him to bring her back into my life.

Looking at the beauty of Taj Mahal you could imagine the beauty of love between Shah Jahan and Mumtaj Mahal, but when I visited Taj Mahal a few years back during my school days, I did not have any girlfriend so I never knew the value of true love and today when I don't have a girlfriend I know the value of true love. Things have changed, time has changed, people have changed, but the feeling of love never does. I had tears in my eyes, but I couldn't let them out as my father did not know about my relationship with Megha and I never wanted him to see me crying for a girl. He is a simple man who is strong and silent and he always wanted me to be a tough guy, because he knows the rule of nature "the fittest survives" and according to him I have to be the fittest. He always tried his best to provide me the best teachings, the best life and the best things which I needed in every sphere of my life.

07th October, 2014 (Delhi)

For last two days I noticed Megha was ignoring my messages and she was avoiding my calls too. Her phone was never busy but she was always online and even then she ignored my messages. I still had her Facebook password and I eventually logged into it; when I went to the messages I realized she has just deleted her chats with a guy, her classmate. I was already frustrated and seeing her misbehaving with me, I doubted whether she was deliberately chatting with people online, to avoid me and trying to divert her mind from me.

I called her and she disconnected the call. I again called her and kept calling her until she received the call. She was angry and I wondered and I asked her, "How you can be so angry with someone whom you loved so madly..." I also asked her the reason for avoiding me, to which she replied that she did not want to talk to me and she just wanted me to avoid having frequent conversations with her. I wondered how could I stop myself from messaging her when she was always online. Coming to the point I asked her the reason behind deleting her chats with her classmates which she recently had. She replied that she was not my girlfriend now and I have no right to ask her this type of question. I couldn't understand why she was behaving like this; I couldn't accept that this was my Megha who was behaving like this. I was confused, is she doing this to change me and make me realize the level of mistakes I have committed or she has really started hating me now.

I burned out in anger and I never had to be angry in front of her. I tried to control myself but I couldn't, I asked her to come on a group chat with the guy with whom she was chatting over FB and she refused to come. But then she sent me the screen shots of a few chats that she had been having with the classmate which clearly proved that it was just a normal chat and they had nothing personal in that. Megha even did not have the phone number of that guy, otherwise they would not have talked over FB.

She was clear, she was true and she was loyal but me, I had again done something which is worst than whatever I did till date. According to her I lost trust in her, and now because she was hurt she disconnected the call saying "It's over, you last chance is over, and now if you call me or message me ill block you from everywhere".

A tear dropped out of my left eye, and then a lot of them from both the eyes. The eyes had started crying since last few months and they didn't know when they are going to stop or they are never going to stop ever. The eye lashes were so heavy and tired to shed tears that every drop of tear looked like a drop of blood, but I could only shed them when I am alone.

Me Without her

08th October, 2014

It was 4 am in the morning when I check for her last seen on Whatsapp, it was 10:59pm and she did not reply to any of my messages, they were still unread. I was frustrated, broken, weak, sad, and emotional and dismantled mentally. I did not have any thoughts running inside my head except her; I was thinking why all of this has happened, where we both went wrong and how I could get her back.

My mom woke up, she noticed me looking at my phone. She knew what was going on in my head and probably she knew that we have again broken up with each other. She asked me what I am looking in the phone, and I started crying. When you are very sad and you have someone who cares the most, you automatically burst out in tears and you have no control over yourself. She wiped my tears and said, "You are a boy, and boys don't cry. You made mistakes but many of them were not much important to focus upon, you tried your best to bring her back and now wait for her, if she truly loves you she will be back, otherwise forget her."

Had anyone else told me those words, I would have done something to him, something which he would never forget, but it was my mom and moms are always know us from inside out and she knew what I was and what I had become now. I know that she always wanted me to be brave and strong; looking at me so weakly she said, "I always thought you were a strong boy. That you never feel very sad for anything and being my child you have to be the strongest because I am strong and I never let people hurt me, be strong and go to sleep now."

I was unlucky to lose Megha; but I was lucky that at the worst time of my life my mom was with me, and god had planned everything perfectly for me. I went to the balcony for a while, I looked at the calm, dark sky, only the moon was lightening the earth and there were no stars. It was as beautiful and inspiring as a painting. It looked like the night itself is sad about me, but there was someone who was ignoring me or was happy to see me like this, god! I looked at the sky again with the red angry eyes filled with tears, and cursed him for giving me so much of pain. If I had a chance to have a word with me I knew I would have made him cry too, but he was hidden behind those dark clouds and he did not came out to see me and help me.

I came back to the room and wrote something on my Facebook Timeline.

Neend uda ke jaati hai khwabon me aake is tarha
Jaise pyar nahi koi gunah kiya ho
Chahat ka teri itna hua asar hum par
Jaise tere bina kabhi hum jiye na ho…

I didn't know when I fell asleep. My mom woke me up, then she went on to the temple. I wanted to stop her from going there, a place where nobody is there to listen to us but she had her own belief and I had my own.

In the afternoon I came to know that I haven't had breakfast since morning and I have been lost somewhere since I woke up. I don't know where I was lost but now I knew, I was at my home with my mom and she had made my all-time favorite Rajasthani food. Whenever a proper Rajasthani meal was made I always used to eat extra, but today I did not wanted to eat anything. All my hunger and thirst was lost, and I was too.

Mom forced me to eat something and it was her duty to do so, I refused to eat but then as I did not wanted her to become sad I had a few bites. Sometimes when I am too happy or too sad my mom feeds me with her own hands and today she was feeding me. With every bite she put into my mouth I missed the day when Megha fed me for the first time in a restaurant and I couldn't resist myself from shedding tears. I wasn't crying but the tears were coming out of my eyes like they were hidden since years and waited to come out.

When someone switched on the TV I wanted him to switch it off, as I was sad and there was nothing which could make me happy or busy. I did not even like to watch my favorite serials on SAB TV. All I was doing is looking at her pictures in my phone and asking her why she left me alone when she had made thousands of promises to be with me forever.

I tried to call her but every time I clicked the green button I disconnected the call before letting it to ring. I knew if I call her, she will not listen to me and she will maybe block me from everywhere.

09th October, 2014

My phone rang, the screen showed "Megha calling", I received the call and it was Megha on the other side, she said she wanted to meet as today she is not going to her college. I said I'll be ready in half an hour and when I am ready I would call her and we will meet at Kohat Enclave Metro Station, our favorite place. When I was ready I called her to reach Kohat and I went to the florist and bought a single red rose for her, she was back into my life and I wanted to welcome her with the Red Rose. I was late this time and she waited for me for 15 minutes but she did not bother as I am rarely late.

She was sitting on the driver's side inside the car and I was sitting next to her, she smiled at me and I smiled at her. We both held each other's hand and then I asked her to close her eyes, she closed her eyes and said, "I know it's a flower." She smiled.

I gave her the flower and she opened her eyes, she liked the flower and smiled at me, then she asked me to close my eyes and I asked her why, she put her fingers on my lips and asked me to close my eyes. I closed my eyes and waited for her to ask me to open up, but she didn't.

I said, "Can I open my eyes now, Megha! Megha!, speak up otherwise I'll open my eyes, ok, I am going to open my eyes at the count of three, 1… 2… and 3."

It was completely dark, I was at my home, and of course shocked. I searched for my cell phone and saw the time, it was 4 am in the morning, mom was awake as I was speaking aloud and thrashing around wildly in the dream. She did not react as she knew I was still in my dream-like state and I turned my face on the opposite side. I was shattered once again, I cannot cry, I cannot shout, and I cannot breathe without her, but I had to.

I turned my face towards my mom and said, "Mom, are you awake?" She said, "Yes, I am, are you not feeling sleepy." I kept my head on her lap, and I wished if I could die that very moment, its heaven to die on mom's lap, but as it says, "Good people die sooner." and I was not among them. Mom knew I was dying inside but all she said is, be strong and trust me this time will fly away very soon.

10th October, 2014 (Back to my Home town)

For a change my mom wanted to take me back home. We had to board a train at 8:45am in the morning, as soon as we settled down in the train; it started taking me away from Megha. I hated this moment specially, when I had to go away from her, although we never meet daily with each other at least our house was in the radius of 3 kms only, and above all we were taking breath in the same air. But I had to go home as everyone else here wanted me to go for a change. They thought may be ill feel better if I go away from Delhi, but I don't think so. I knew it is going to make it ever worst than before. I walked to the washroom in the train and dialed Megha's number, and then realized she is not my girlfriend anymore and she is not going to pick up the call, I disconnected and went back to my seat.

My eyes were filled with expectations that she will be back and my heart was filled with pain of losing her, alas I couldn't cry all the time and tell people about what has happened to me. I kept my tears hidden all the way to hometown and finally we reached home. As usual Lovika, my cousin little sister came out running towards me and sat on my lap. She smiled at me and asked me, "How are you *bhaiya?*", I hugged her and whispered in her ears, pray to god that Megha comes back; your brother will be fine again. She did not understand anything and she smiled at me running towards my mom.

My depression was killing me but I had to bear all the things alone, I hated when someone is watching some serial or movies based on love stories, but I couldn't stop anyone here because they don't know about my relationship with Megha and I never wanted to tell them. I tried to play hide and seek with my siblings but after a point of time I couldn't. While hiding behind the stairs I realized I am hiding from the reality that she has left me alone. I was very difficult for me to spend time at my home town now and with the passage of time it became more difficult when my local friends asked me about Megha's well-being and our relationship, and when I had to tell them about all those things which happened till now and then realizing that they too are with me but they said to me, "Leave her!"

12th October, 2014

I was lost somewhere, and that somewhere was where she was. Of course I did not have anything in mind except for the relationship, its complications, and the breakup which I believed was not actually a breakup. It was in the evening when I was roaming on my terrace and was wondering how life changes in no time, there was a day when I used to come to the terrace and talk to her over the phone, and everybody at home knew that I was hiding in the terrace to talk to someone and they never showed me that they knew everything. But on a day like today when I had no one to talk to, suddenly everybody at home realized that I am alone and they were here with me on the terrace to accompany me.

This is what we call a lovable family; where they know you inside out and they help you without expressing anything directly to you. I was getting a strong gut feeling that something unusual is going to happen, Megha was going to come back or something bad was going to happen to me. But I ignored my sixth sense as though I was not in my senses and I want something to happen to me that's why I am feeling it.

Suddenly Dinesh, my brother shouted, "*Bhai* dinner is ready, come to the kitchen please."

I did not want to eat but because I was at my home I had to. So, I went to the stairs running.

Bash!!...

"Oh he is hit badly, wait... wait... he is bleeding, let's take him to the hospital he is becoming unconscious..." I was unable to move, I couldn't open my eyes and I could see only red color with my closed eyes and there was complete silence now.

13th October, 2014

"Are you okay now, I think he is gaining consciousness, yes he is opening his eyes and trying to look around, thank god! he has gained consciousness..."

"Doctor is he fine now?"

"He is still not out of danger, but we hope he will be fine soon."

"Wait he is getting unconscious again. Ck, Ck? Open your eyes."

14th October, 2014

"Open your eyes *bhai* its Megha on the call, she wants to talk to you."

I almost jumped off the bed and saw that it was Preeti, my cousin sitting beside me and she handed me her cell phone and said, "Talk to Megha, she is worried about you."

"Hello! Hello!"

"Hello."

"Are you okay?"

"Yes, I am. How are you?"

"I am not fine and how I can be, when my sweetheart is lying on a hospital bed. I am so sorry, please get well soon..." she started crying.

"I was now feeling heavy and I started crying too."

Preeti took that phone away and she walked out of the room.

I wanted to stop her and talk to Megha but I was feeling drowsy and it was all blank once again.

16th October, 2014

"Good morning *Bhai*, how are you feeling today?"

"Good morning Preeti, I am fine. But what the hell has happened to me? Why I am hospitalized?

"Oh! You slipped in the stairs and got a head injury, after which you became unconscious and you were taken to the hospital and now you are doing fine. You are recovering."

"Did I talk to Megha yesterday? I mean was it a dream or it was real?"

"Yes Bhai, it was real. In fact she wants to talk to you let me call her."

I saw my mom was standing outside the room and she was looking at me with a question in her eyes, she was wondering "Will he die for that girl?"

I couldn't look at her and I turned my eyes toward Preeti again, she handed over the cell phone to me.

"Oye! *Ab thik hoja na jaldi se,* I want you back baby. You know na how much I Love you. Please *jaldi se thik hoja... tu sun raha hai na*?"

"Hmm... *sun raha hu*, ill get well soon and will be back to Delhi very soon to meet you. I have been dying without you sweet heart, **I Love you**..."

"I Love you too."

"Wait! Megha he is getting unconscious again, I'll call you later. Bye!"

17th October, 2014

"How are you beta?"

"I am fine Mom, how are you?"

"I will be fine. When you will be back home?"

"Don't worry mom, it's just a small head injury I'll be back home soon."

"Mausi! Dinesh is calling you outside, the doctor has allowed me to talk to him for a while," Monika didi said.

"Alright," my mom kissed me on my forehead and went outside the room.

"Hi! Bhai, *Kaisa hai ab*?"

"*Thik hoon*, how are you?"

"*Bas tu jaldi thik hoja hum sab theek ho jaenge...*"

I smiled at Monika Di, she asked me if I wanted to talk to Megha.

I took my cell phone which she had, I check my Whatsapp and there were a lot of messages from Megha.

"*Babu, jaldi thik ho, mai tera wait kar rahi hu...*"

"I am dying to see you, please get well soon..."

"I Love you, please come back soon and I'll never go away from you now..."

"*Jab* message *padho*, please smile and miss me a lot..."

"I have told *Bhagwan ji, ki mujhe bimar kar do par meri Jaan ko thik kar do jaldi se...*"

"I am sorry, you are the best, I Love you a lot *shona* get well soon..."

I called her.

She picked up the phone on the first ring and said, "I was waiting for your call, tell me how are you and if you are missing me or not!"

"I am fine, and I am missing you a lot, now when you are back I'll be fine soon."

"Hello! Megha, Monika this side. Doctor said if he will remain conscious for the next 24 hours, we can take him home. He is not allowed to talk on the phone so, I have to disconnect your call. Sorry..."

"I Love you," I shouted over the phone.

She asked Monika di to pass me a flying kiss.

I am damn happy today, she is back, she is back, she is back, yippee...

"*Ab tujhe neend to aaegi nahi, aur tu kal tak hosh me bhi rahega, and kal tu discharge bhi ho jaega,*" Monika didi said smiling at me.

"Di! Tell me one thing, who informed Megha about my accident and how did she come back to me?"

"Preeti called her. She informed her about your accident, she told her how you were behaving since last few days and I also tried to convince her that you are incomplete without her and you need her badly in your life. She said she never wanted to hurt you; she always loved you and wanted you to prove yourself and bring her back into your life."

"She said you are a nice man but you are equally bad when you are angry, and she hated this about you. She broke up with you to make you realize that your anger can only burn your relationship; in the future you have to learn to delete possessiveness and anger from your life if you want her back, but when she realized that you are so madly in love with her that you actually met an accident while thinking about her all the times, she took a chance and came back for you..."

"Now when she is back, you have to prove her that you will now change for her; that you will be a better man, you will love her more and care for her more. And especially that you will never get angry with her and will never shout on her. Do you understand? You will never be possessive and will always support her instead of asking her questions. She has given you a chance as a friend once again and you cannot ask her to come back to the relationship until she is ready for it..."

"But Di! She said **I Love you** to me..."

"Yes I know, she loves you, but she says when you are back home, you have to start analyzing your mistakes and change yourself so that she doesn't have to break it again and she will be back forever when she realizes that you are a changed man..."

"Okay! I'll try my best Di."

She smiled at me and left the room, it was night time so the lights were off in a few minutes and I was waiting for the next day so that I could go home and talk to Megha.

18th October, 2014

I was awake whole night thinking about what all I have to do and wondering when I could go back home. In the morning the paper work got completed and after all the formalities I was free to go home.

But the most important thing was that my love, my Megha was back now and I loved her so much that to get her back in my life I thought that I am ready to get hospitalized for the rest of my life.

Finally, I was back home. I called her up, and she was happy to know about my well-being. I promised her that everything was going to be fine now and she need not worry about me anymore. I hung up as everybody at my home was around me and they were taking extra care of me. My cute little sister Lovika was with me the whole time, I don't know what was going inside her head but she was showing intense care for me. She asked me to switch off the mobile as the doctor has advised me not to take stress. I was wondering if she even knew the meaning of stress, but I go surprised when she took my phone and kept it under the pillow and asked me to lay down and take rest. The innocence of a small child could make you happy at the worst time of your life.

20th October, 2014 (Monika Di's House)

After getting a checkup done in the hospital, I went to Monika Di's house which was on the way. In the evening me, my cousins Deepika Di and Saurabh, went to have some 'Gol Gappas' in the market. We were having fun by taking some funny photographs of each other and suddenly I saw a beautiful girl coming towards us. Everyone started looking at her and I was trying to remember who she was. When she came closer I realized she was Anamika, who met me in Deepika Di's Marriage a year back and we became very good friends in no time, but I had not had any conversation with her since last 9 months as our friendship did not last for more than 3 months.

She came to me and said 'Hi' to me. I knew she was going to talk to me and everyone around us got surprised to know that we knew each other. Imagine a situation where people are dying to take an autograph from Katrina Kaif and she comes to you... you will feel like a celebrity. Anamika was nothing less than the Katrina of that town and everyone got jealous of me as she was talking to me and ignoring everybody else there.

Tough we met after a long time and we had some unsolved problems between us. We met each other like nothing had happened between us. I asked her if she would like to have some 'Gol Gappas' with us, but she said she had to buy some stuff from the market so she would have to leave. She left for the market and soon we were back to Monika Di's house.

In the evening my Facebook messenger gave me a message, which was from Anamika. She said it's been long time since we haven't talked to each other and she was surprised to see me in her town today and I was surprised too that she was back in my life at this stage where everything was messed up and was unstable. We became friends again by adding each other on Facebook and I was confused on all the things which were happening to me.

21st October, 2015

Megha was busy in visiting her relatives as during the festival season; in Agarwal families we have a trend of giving a lot of gifts and sweets to the daughters and sisters of our family, especially those daughters and sisters who are married. We rarely had time to talk to each other but it was okay, as we also needed to give a break to each other so that the wounded relationship could heal.

Anamika and I did not exchange phone numbers as we never wanted to get back to the situation where we have been a year back. Let me take you to the flash back.

(November 2014) My Mom and I were attending Deepika Di's marriage; Anamika is the daughter of my mom's friend and also a relative of Deepika Di. She was invited by Deepika Di's family to attend the marriage. Anamika was looking very beautiful in her golden anarkali style kurta with her long black hair. Her smile was her most dazzling ornament and she was perfect at giving it to others. Of course when you are in a relationship you cannot fall in love with every girl; something which you can do only when you are single. She was attractive and everyone was constantly looking at her only.

While she was sitting besides Preeti Di and Mom in front of Me, Deepika di and few others, Preeti di suggested to my mom that she get me married to Anamika as she was the most beautiful girl out there. But my mom refused and said she was not the prefect one for my son. I was surprised to see that a beautiful girl got rejected by my mom and that too on her face, so directly.

After the marriage I saw her on my list of Facebook mutual friends and sent her a friend request which she accepted. Her first message to me was, "Why did your mom reject me?" and I had no answer for it. I said, "I don't know but maybe there is no reason behind rejecting you…" mischievously.

Such chats with each other as strangers to each other and that too so comfortably made us good friends in no time. We started chatting over Wechat, and sometimes over the phone too. She started caring for me like a best friend and I was happy that she cared for me. She was a good person and she used to ask me all the normal things which a 'Best Friend' would ask and I did not have any problem with that. I liked everything in her and I thought she was perfect in everything and in every way. She also liked me and thought I was a perfect guy, within a month she knew me inside out but she could never know that I had a girlfriend and I did not realize that a sort of infatuation was developing between us.

Megha knew about my friendship with Anamika and she never realized that I am getting inclined towards her, but she still trusted me. She knew that no matter how much love and care some other girl had for me, no matter how far I may go with that some other girl, in the end I would be back with her and will always be hers only. This is called true Love, when you trust your partner so much so that he/ she doesn't have the guts to leave you no matter whatever has happened or happens. Her trust on me made me realize that I was on the wrong path and I blocked Anamika from everywhere and had no chats with her till we met once again after one year.

Coming back to the present, I got a message on Facebook from Anamika. "Hey! Where have you been since last one year, I mean you was not available on

Wechat, you also removed me from Facebook and also changed your mobile number too. I tried a lot to contact you but could not, why did you do that?"

"Hi! I did not go anywhere, I just did not wanted to talk to you anymore. That's why I deregistered myself from Wechat and removed you from my Facebook friend's list too. The reason being very simple. I felt that I was getting very close to you and I started to develop somewhat of an infatuation. I was in a relationship with a girl for the last 5 years and she trusted me blindly; being in a relationship I can have good and even the best of friends but I had no rights to get into any other relationship than that," I told her.

"You did not tell me that you had a girlfriend, but did you tell her about me? Did she know that we were very close to each other and you started getting inclined towards me?"

"She knows that we had a very close friendship with each other, but she never knew that I was getting inclined towards you. I wanted to tell her many times that I was doing something which she never wanted me to do but I couldn't tell as I wanted to get over it on my own and I did."

"It's good that you did not cheat your girlfriend and you stopped talking to me, but now I don't want to be in any contact with you as I think you lied to me. You did not tell me about you relationship with Megha and you also left me in between."

"I don't know the reason for not telling you about my relationship with Megha," I told her, "But I certainly left you in between and I accept that. But when we met again I just did not wanted to keep you in dark and that's why

I have told you the truth. My relationship with Megha has met many ups and downs these last few months and I don't want it to get back to being bad again. So I have decided I will not hide anything from her after my relationship with her is back into the track once. I know you are hurt and you may not talk to me hereafter but I want you to be with me as I definitely need all my good friends to be with me."

"You stopped talking to me! You did you even think about me, did you even bother to think how I was worried about you? Why do you expect that I should now stay in your life?"

"I stopped talking to you to save my relationship with Megha, and being a girl you understand that. I stopped talking to you because I love Megha more than anything else in this world and I did not wanted to see myself going the wrong way. But today my relationship with her is going through the worst period ever and I need all my friends to be with me as you are amongst the best buddies I have ever had."

"Sorry, my heart was always with you and is with you as you are a true person heart but my mind is not allowing me to talk to you. So I just need a break and I wish everything becomes good between you and Megha... bye, hope to see you again somewhere at some point of time in lives."

22nd October, 2014

I wished Megha a 'Happy Diwali' through Whatsapp but she replied disinterestedly after few hours. I called her but she was very reluctant to pick up the call, maybe she was busy I thought but I never knew the reason behind her not picking up the phone call. I then waited for her call but as the time passed by my frustration increased and in the evening I called her again when she picked up the call but she said she did not want to talk to me and disconnected the call which was unexpected as everything was solved between us and there was no reason for her to get angry on me now.

Despite calling her again and again she did not picked up the call, meanwhile Preeti Di called me up to wish me 'Happy Diwali' and she asked me the reason for sounding so sad. I explained everything to her and she said she would have a word with Megha and she had a con call with her and I. When Di asked her the reason for behaving so indifferently she replied that she had read all the chats between Anamika and me on Facebook.

She said she was ready to forgive me for everything I had done till now, and she was ready to get back in the relationship as soon as she felt everything was going to heal. She said that she had a lot of trust in me and she loved me very much, but she never knew that I would hide the fact about me getting inclined towards Anamika from her, though it was not intentional. I stopped talking to Anamika as soon as I realized that I was going the wrong way but I shouldn't have hidden this thing from Megha. She said she never wanted to know anything like this and she was badly hurt and this was the end of the relationship from her side as she had lost all the hopes, trust and feelings she had for me.

Preeti di and I tried everything to make her understand until Monika di called me up and I had to tell her everything and she too got involved. She convinced Megha by telling her that everything was getting worse just to test our love and relationship and that you (Megha) are going to fail if you leave. She did not want to get into the relationship but still she said she would be my friend till she made her final decision.

The 'Happy Diwali' turned into a pathetic Diwali; destiny did not look into my favor, and the girl who was out of my life for last one year came back for a few days. But alas, it did not end as I had hoped, prayed and expected...

10th November, 2014

I was back to Delhi, My health was getting worse because of depression. My Mamaji and Mami decided to call Megha to their house so that they can have a chat with her and try to figure out what could be done. I had hope and I thought may be everything would be okay, but she came with her final decision which did not change even when she knew everything was just unintentional and it all out to be the worst day by day of my life. I looked into her eyes, they were sad, her eyes explained that innocently she wanted to help me and to hold my hand but she could not., she was worried about me but she did not want to come back, her actions did not match her words, her body language was completely opposite to her behavior.

She said she to me that she didn't want to come back to the relationship and to me, that she doesn't even want to be friends with me as it would put me in a situation where I would keep loving her and she will have no such feelings for me. She said it would be more hurtful if it became a one sided relationship and I would not be able to move on. She knew that everything was against the relationship and maybe it will get to the worst, she had no positive thoughts and she had no hope that everything would be fine.

She looked into my eyes and said, "If you truly love me, set me free, if you really want me to be happy, don't force me to come back. The day I feel that you have changed and I should get back to the relationship, I will." These words were not hers, they seemed to be put forcefully in her mouth, and she said something which her eyes couldn't support. It was an untold reason which she knew but I didn't, I asked her several times for the reason behind her decision but she couldn't tell me one except few words, "Your nature."

While she was going back to her car through the stairs, I called her name, she looked back at me. I asked her to come up and give me a hug, she came up without a second thought, she hugged me and said take care, her eyes were filled with tears but she tried to hide them. I said to her, "I will wait for you." To which she replied, "Don't do that." She left me once again but I hoped that she would be back.

I still love you and will love you till the end
My heart has paused, like the deserts wet sand
I know you are the only one, my one and only friend
We both are broken but, it's not the only end
People live and die but we are meant to live forever
Maybe not in bodies, but in the souls till the end
I still miss you and will miss you till the end
The years have passed and I will wait for more thousand
The time flies away, and with it flies away my thoughts
Feelings remain the same, same till the end
I will wait for the time which has passed
The time together we have spent
The life goes on, and so does the journey
But you will always be special no matter what has happened
I will always be yours, and will be yours till the end
I still love you and will love you till the end.